thinandbeautiful.com

thinandbeautiful.com

Liane Shaw

Second Story Press

Library and Archives Canada Cataloguing in Publication

Shaw, Liane, 1959-

Thinandbeautiful.com / by Liane Shaw.

ISBN 978-1-897187-62-3

1. Anorexia nervosa--Juvenile fiction. I. Title. II. Title: Thin and beautiful .com.

PS8637.H3838T55 2009   jC813'.6   C2009-903079-9

Edited by Yasemin Ucar
Copyedited by Alison Kooistra
Cover and text design by Melissa Kaita
Cover photo by istockphoto

Printed and bound in Canada

Second Story Press gratefully acknowledges the support of the Ontario Arts Council and the Canada Council for the Arts for our publishing program. We acknowledge the financial support of the Government of Canada through the Book Publishing Industry Development Program.

Published by
SECOND STORY PRESS
20 Maud Street, Suite 401
Toronto, Ontario, Canada
M5V 2M5
www.secondstorypress.ca

For my two beautiful daughters,
Ashlee and Steff, who inspired me
to write this story, and for Carolyn,
who always believed that I would.

March 13

It's morning again. I can tell because the sun came up. It keeps doing that, whether I want it to or not.

I used to like mornings...or so I'm told. I don't really remember. My mother tells me that I used to be a morning person. I'm not a morning person now. I'm not a night person either. I don't know what kind of person I am. Maybe I'm just a person without a time – or a place. Or maybe I'm not a person at all. I should go outside and see if I still have a shadow.

I won't be going anywhere until I do what I'm told like a good little girl. Everyone here has to come up with some sort of lame personal goal they have to aim for before they can get out of here. Kind of like a get-out-of-jail-free card, but it isn't really free because you have to work for it. I couldn't think of anything remotely interesting so the obnoxiously cheerful redhead with the clipboard, who thinks she's an expert on everything completely unimportant, told me I had to write down my memories and my feelings. How do you write a feeling?

Anyway, I'm doing what she said because I figure they'll let me out of this dump sooner if I look like I'm trying to do what they ask me to do. I look on it as kind of a game where no one knows the rules but me. That way, I'm sure I'll win. I just haven't totally figured out how yet. I do know what the big prize is, though. Freedom.

I still can't believe I actually ended up here. My parents talked about it a couple of times when they thought I was out of earshot, but I never thought they would actually do it. I mean, it's not like I'm some kind of criminal or something who needs to be locked away for the protection of society. I'm also not some kind of nutcase who pops pills or decorates her arms with slash marks. I know some kids like that. There was once this girl at my school who asked me if I wanted to see something cool. I said sure, why not? So she takes me into the auditorium, because she's one of those audiovisual club geeks, and looks around to make sure no one is there. I look around, too, like we're in some bizarre detective movie and we're bank robbers checking for cops. I don't know what I thought she was going to show me, but I've got to admit that I was pretty freaked when she rolled up her sleeves to show off a bunch of little round scars and big red lines all over her arms. I asked her what happened and she told me she had done it to herself with cigarettes and a utility knife. I thought I was going to puke, but I didn't. I just shook my head and walked away. I didn't know what to say to her. I couldn't figure out why she showed it to me in the first place. I didn't tell anyone about it. Maybe I should have told someone about it.

I wonder what happened to her. I don't remember seeing her around much after that. Maybe she ended up in a place like this. Hey, maybe she's here. I should look for her. It would be nice to see a familiar face.

I mean, I know she isn't really here. It's just that someone like her probably needs to be in a dump like this where she's locked up so she can't hurt herself. I'm not like her. I didn't do anything to deserve being stuck in here. But they locked me up anyway and threw away the key. Actually, it's even worse than that. They locked me up and took away my Internet. My whole lifeline to everyone and anyone who matters is floating away in cyberspace. The only Internet access in this social black hole is down in some office where we prisoners aren't allowed to go. One of these nights, I'm going to find a way to get down there. This is a free country after all. I have a right to the Internet. I'm sure it's in the Constitution.

It's bizarre. I mean, really, why would anyone waste time making some fancy private treatment prison for people who just want to look good? I didn't think that was a crime but I ended up here anyway. I didn't even get my day in court. I was arrested and convicted by my parents and my mental-case doctor without any chance to tell my side at all.

chapter 1

Maybe this whole memory-writing thing isn't such a bad idea after all. At least I'll get to tell my story to someone – even if it's only to myself. So, here it goes.

The story of my life, by Madison J. Nessfield.

OK, so I lied. I'm not going to write down the story of my life. First of all, I don't have it all sitting in my head. I mean, I have lots of pieces of it, like an endless stream of thirty-second commercials running through my brain. I don't even know if all of the pieces are actually real or if I pulled them from pictures and home movies. I don't remember a lot of the details either. It's more like I have black-and-white pictures in my brain and I have to fill in the colors with my imagination. It doesn't matter much, I guess. I just need to figure out which memories I should be trying to remember, so I can keep everyone happy and make it look like I'm trying to figure out my life. I don't even know where to start. I guess at the beginning.

My earliest memory is from when I was three and I had just

wet my pants outside in my driveway. Nice, eh? I had wanted to ride my trike so much that I just kind of lost track of time and all of a sudden there's this yellow puddle on my seat. I was totally petrified that I was going to get yelled at because I was too stupid to run in to the bathroom. I got up and started bawling like a complete baby. All of a sudden I felt these arms around me, and I was being picked up. My friend's mom had me in this bear hug and was telling me that everything was all right. She probably got all wet and gross, but she didn't even care. She made me feel like everything was all right. No one yelled at me at all.

Flash ahead. Now I'm like six, and I've graduated to a two-wheeler. I had those dinky little training wheel deals on the bike for almost the whole summer, and then I decided I was ready to go it alone. My mom said she'd hold the seat so I could balance. So there I was, sitting all proud on my pink seat on my even pinker bike, and my mom started running and pushing me down the sidewalk while I pumped my legs like a maniac, trying to move on my own. She's all panting and puffing and I'm yelling at her to let go. So she did, and I fell flat on my butt with my pretty pink bike on top of me. My mom tried to help me up, and I slapped at her hand and did it myself. My dad joined the party and tried to hold the seat so I could try it again, but I slapped him too. Nice kid. Anyway, I kept climbing on and falling down and getting ticked at the people trying to help me up until I finally managed to wobble my way down the sidewalk. I just had to do it my own way. Your own way is always the best way. It's hard to do something wrong if you made it up in the first place.

Next clip, kindergarten. My buddy Annie and I used to walk to kindergarten every day by ourselves. Well, that's not really true. In my mind we were alone, but my mom reminded me a few years ago that we were always being followed by a couple of grade eight kids who lived on our street and made a few bucks a week watching us hike to school. I guess it wasn't too far from our house, but it seemed like miles and miles to us, with our short little kid legs. The day was a rainy one so Annie and I had on these little yellow raincoats that we thought were wonderful, but probably made us look like mutated ducks. We had rubber boots on, too, which gave us instant permission to jump in all of the puddles. The boots always got full of water, but we didn't care. It was kind of fun to dump them out and make new puddles inside the house.

Annie decided that we needed to do something different than puddle jumping on the way to school that day. She got the brilliant idea that worm collecting was a much better use of our time. At least, in my memory it was her idea. I don't remember any of this being my fault. I wasn't even sure if I wanted to pick the squiggly little guys up or not, but Annie persuaded me that her mother was in desperate need of worms for her garden. I had loved Annie's mother madly ever since the whole pants-peeing incident, so I reluctantly, but bravely, agreed. It was more fun than I had thought it would be, and we managed to pretty much fill the big square pockets on our fancy yellow coats with piles of squirming, stinking, desperate worms.

It didn't occur to either of us to wonder what the worms were going to do all morning while we learned our ABCs from the tall and terrifying MRS. FINDLAY. I put her name in capitals because when I remember her she is always larger than life. She looked about ten feet tall to us. She always made me think of a scary dragon that terrorized the townspeople in a book my brother read to me once when my mom wasn't listening. Man, that book scared me for weeks! The dragon was huge and ferocious and ate little children for breakfast. MRS. FINDLAY looked at us in the exact same way that the dragon in the book looked at the children it wanted to have as appetizers. In my memory, she even looks like a dragon, with greenish-gray skin and big teeth. I seem to remember long, red fingernails that could have been claws covered in fresh blood from some poor, unsuspecting cow that she had eaten for dessert. She was very strict and always wanted the classroom kept really neat and tidy, just like the dragon, who picked the bones of his victims sparkling clean so that his cave wouldn't get messed up. We learned quickly that we had better always clean up after ourselves at school and carefully hang our coats up in the cloakroom on the proper hook, making sure that our boots were lined up underneath the little bench.

So that's exactly what Annie and I did on that rainy day. We carefully hung our coats on the proper hook. It was a little hard to do because they were heavier than usual, but we managed it. Then we took off our boots and put on our shoes, careful not to make puddles on MRS. FINDLAY'S floor – floor puddles were saved for home, where our mothers just shook their heads and mopped them up. Satisfied that we had met the required standards of kindergarten cleanliness, we went to our seats to become brilliant.

We were, understandably, completely shocked about an

hour later when MRS. FINDLAY threw a complete and total hissy fit.

"Who put these...these things here!" she yelled, standing in the cloakroom. I'm not really sure if that's what she actually yelled, but it was something like that. We all froze in our seats, shaking in our shoes and wondering what the heck she was talking about. She came out of the cloakroom, with her face all red and kind of shiny looking. Her eyes were bugging out of her head like some kind of maniac insect and she seemed to be having trouble breathing. Her dragon teeth were glistening with saliva, which was threatening to drip down onto the floor. We cowered in fear, certain that she was going to start breathing fire at any moment.

"What is this?" she asked, holding up a worm that was desperately trying to escape her evil clutches.

"It's a worm," Bobby Smith said helpfully. I made up his name. It's close enough.

"I know it's a worm! I want to know how it got in my cloakroom!" She looked around at our terrified faces, her eyes boring into our tiny brains. We couldn't run, we couldn't hide! We also couldn't talk, so we just sat there with our tongues glued to the insides of our mouths.

"Did you do this?" she glared at me with eyes like lasers. I shook my head. Annie shook her head too, even though MRS. FINDLAY wasn't even looking at her. I think that's what gave us away. That, and the fact that the worms were busily crawling out of the pockets of two little yellow coats with Annie and Madison labels stitched carefully into the collars.

We didn't get eaten, and no one got burned. But we did

have our first detention that day. We didn't even know what the word meant, but we knew it was pretty bad. It came with a note that we had to take home to our parents. We couldn't read yet, so we didn't know what horrors the mishmash of ABCs contained. I was kind of surprised when I showed my mom the note and she laughed about it. I didn't think that having a dragon for a teacher was very funny. I never did find out what the note said.

Annie and I were best friends from that day forward, bonded for life by a mutual fear of dragons. When we got a little older, we stopped being afraid of them and developed a kind of obsession with them. We bought each other dragon stuff for years on every birthday and Christmas and any other occasion we could come up with. I have practically every size, shape, and color of dragon you could imagine.

Annie and I aren't friends anymore, though. I think she's part of the reason I'm in this place. I guess the bond wasn't for life after all.

I wonder if she kept all her dragons.

March 16

One of the nameless horde of prison guards just came in to give me my protein shake. That's what they call it. Isn't that a joke? They tell me it isn't fattening or anything, that it's just full of vitamins, nutrients, and vegetable juice. Yum. I know they're lying. It's thick and gross and disgusting, and I can tell it has more calories in it than a McD's triple-thick shake. I have to drink it, though. If I don't, I'll get solitary confinement. That means I would have to sit in this little room where they'd have someone watching my every move. They'll take me away from everything I have that makes me feel a little bit like me.

Not that I have much in this place – a few books, my CD player, a pillow that I brought from home that has a dragon embroidered on it. I think Annie gave it to me, so I guess I shouldn't have brought it. Anyway, it's comfortable, but I bet I wouldn't be allowed to have it with me, because they'd likely think I was going to put it over my face and suffocate myself. I bet they wouldn't even let me take my writing stuff in case I write myself to death. All I'd be left with is thinking. I don't really like to think for extended periods of time. It makes my brain hurt. Not hurt as in physical pain, like a headache. It's just that there seems to be too much to think about. My body, my parents, my friends, my weight, my school, what to eat, when to exercise, how to get out of here, why my life sucks.... It's like my thoughts start moving too fast and filling up all of the empty spaces so that I can't separate them from each other. I literally can't think straight, because I don't have room to keep them organized. The pressure builds until I feel like I might explode if one more thought tries to squeeze in there, so I try to make them all go away. The problem is that the more I try not to think, the more I think about thinking, which starts to make me feel basically nuts. So, thinking is not really my favorite sport.

So, I take the proteins and suck them back like a model prisoner, which I am. But they're not as smart as they think they are. I have unsupervised bathroom privileges because I've been such a good girl, so the protein shake can always visit

Mr. Toilet when no one is around. I can do it with no sound at all, so even if Big Red and her squad of bathroom police are listening outside the door, they figure I'm just doing what people do in the can. It's my game. Madison, one – Redheaded Demon, zero.

chapter 2

I can't believe it took me a whole chapter to get up to kindergarten. The good news is that the rest of my childhood, up until I hit the whole teen thing, is mostly one boring run-on sentence, with blurred images here and there. I don't even bother with thirty-second commercial memories – more like five-second sound bites. I do remember being a nerd-baby in school. I wanted to be the smartest and never quite managed it. I would always wait when the tests or report cards were handed out, sure that this time I would be the number one geek. But there was always someone with one mark higher. Come to think of it, it was always the same someone. I hated her for years, and now I can't even remember her name. Weird.

Annie was always so much cooler than me about everything. She was super smart but didn't feel the need to show it off. Annie was actually named by her grandmother, who was a big fan of the book *Anne of Green Gables*. Annie has her grandma's Japanese copy of the book and she brought it to school and tried to read a bit to us, but she didn't really know all that much Japanese so it was kind of funny. Annie even reminds me of Anne, all strong willed and creative and full of answers. Except that Annie's hair is black instead of red. She did try to dye it once just to see what she would look like, but it turned out kind of mud-colored. If it had been me, I would have dyed it back to black before anyone saw me, but she left it that way. She never seemed to really care what people thought about her. There's this expression I've heard about marching to your own drummer. That's what Annie has always been able to do. She has her own music playing in her head, and the sounds from the people outside never manage to drown it out. The music in my head always has the volume turned down so low that I can't hear my own music over everyone else's.

Music. Now, that's something I do remember. I played the piano from the time I could read. My first piano lessons were in the lunchroom in my elementary school, and we all sat at the lunch tables with cardboard cutouts of the keyboard. There was only one piano and maybe twelve kids or so, so we all had to wait for our two-minute turn on the real deal. I loved it from day one. We had an old player piano at home that you could pedal with your feet and make amazing songs come out. I used to sit on my dad's knee and try to hit the pedals when I was little. I remember being so excited the first time I managed it on my own. It was easy to get excited back then, I guess.

A few years later, I got the chance to play on a real grand piano in a music studio my piano teacher rented for our annual recital downtown. On the day of the concert, I spent equal time trying to improve my piano playing and trying to improve my appearance. I had this theory that I would play better if I looked good. About an hour before we were due to leave the house, I put on my best outfit and went to the bathroom to inspect myself in the mirror and see if I looked pretty enough to play beautiful music.

And that's when I saw it.

Huge, red, and ready to ooze. An angry volcano sitting in the middle of my right cheek, pulsing with the fires of the earth's core. I could see it throbbing steadily, preparing to erupt. I could almost feel the lava coursing down my face and dripping off my chin. I could only imagine the crater that would be left behind, a gaping hole where I once had a face!

I ran to the bathroom, hand held tightly against my cheek, trying desperately to hold back nature's fury. There had to be something I could do! Something that could make my face come back again. Then I remembered. Steve. He was old, almost three years older than me. He was almost fifteen. He might have something that could tame the beast before I had to show my face in public.

"Steve!" I yelled, running down the hall. "I need your help!"

"Why are you holding your face? Is it falling off?" My brother thinks he has a sense of humor. He is alone in that opinion.

"I have a facial problem. I need some cream or something. You must have something."

"Move your hand so I can see."

"No! Just give me something to make it go away!"

Steve rolled his eyes and came over to try and pry my hand away, but I was too quick for him. Or so I thought for about thirty seconds until he caught up with me and managed to pull my hand away from my face. He stood back, still holding my hand so I couldn't run and hide, and stared at me intently.

"Oh," he finally said, after what seemed like hours. "You have a zit. Wow, is it your first one? Starting young, are you? Would you like some zit stuff? I will get that for you." He patted me on the head like a puppy and walked over to his dresser.

"A zit! You make it sound so small! Look at me!" This couldn't be defined with only three letters! Something this big deserved at least half the alphabet! "I can't go to the concert!"

"Maddie, get over yourself. You have a small zit – sorry, pimple – on your cheek. It will most likely be gone by tomorrow. You can hide it, anyway. Ask Mom for some makeup or something. You are seriously out of your strange little mind." He turned his back on me and went back to his computer.

I took the bottle he gave me, read the directions carefully, and put the cream on my face. The bump still looked totally disgusting and the bottle said it could take up to a week to cure it. I didn't want to ask Mom for makeup because I was pretty sure she wouldn't have any, and even if she did, she would say I was too young to wear it and that pimples were a normal part of growing up. That was the kind of thing my mom said about a lot of the stuff I tried to talk to her about. Looking back, I guess it was mostly kid stuff, like friend troubles and school and hair starting to grow in strange places, but it all seemed important to me at the time. I was pretty sure pimples would fall under her category of normal.

Annie didn't wear makeup and she didn't seem to have anything strange and new developing on her face yet, so I couldn't really ask her either. It figures that if I was going to be better and faster than Annie at something, it would be growing pimples!

So, I went to the concert, pimple prominently displayed on my cheek, and played my piece as badly as I had ever played it. My teacher was disappointed and didn't seem too impressed with my explanation. She just didn't see the connection between my cheek and my fingers. I told my mother that my teacher was disappointed in me and that I felt disappointed in myself. Mom said that I shouldn't worry about it and that dealing with disappointment was a normal part of growing up. Then she mentioned that I had a pimple on my cheek and asked me if I wanted to borrow some cover-up when we got home.

March 20

I can't believe it! They caught me! How could they possibly know? I am the champion of garbage removal. No fingers down the throat, no gross noises. Nothing. I've practiced for ages. I can't believe they just walked in and caught me. Is there no privacy in this place? Obviously not. Score one point for the Redheaded Demon of the Ward.

So now my whole good girl image is in the toilet along with the stupid protein shake. I can't believe this place! What did I do to deserve this? I'm going to be sitting in this room forever if this keeps up. I'm on what they call an "individualized schedule," meaning I'm a pain in their collective butts and I'm not out with all the model prisoners doing fun things like circle time and group discussions. I'd rather have my teeth pulled one at a time than be part of the gang mentality around here, but if I don't persuade them of what a good girl I am and join their little pseudo-community, I don't know if I'll ever get out of this place. It's like we graduate from one level to another here. I wonder if there's a ceremony. A cap and gown would be nice. Especially as, at this rate, I don't think I'll be graduating from high school any time soon! Anyway, most people start on the individual schedule, which means we have private counseling and work mostly in our own space. We exercise with a worker standing there keeping watch and eat on our own, with our own customized diet.

They like to think that they give us choices here and they keep telling me I can join the group schedule when I feel ready. They really mean that I can join when I show them that I am behaving myself according to their rules. I don't like their rules.

So they can just wait because I'm not ready to play the game their way yet. There has to be a way out of this place without doing what they want me to do.

chapter 3

When I was a little girl, I used to think my mom knew pretty much everything. She was the one who told me what I needed to know about life. She taught me things like how to ride my bike and swim, and she helped me with my homework. I thought that she had all of the answers. The older I got, though, the less she seemed to understand about real life. My real life, anyway. It's not that she was mean or anything like those evil mothers you see on TV. She was just sort of off in her own space. Motherland, where everything made sense to her in her own mind and she didn't think she had to look inside mine. She couldn't see what bothered me or scared me or embarrassed me anymore, even when I tried to tell her. Like the day she took me to buy my first bra.

When my body decided to make its journey from kidhood to adolescence, the first thing that decided to "blossom" was my chest. That's the polite way of saying that I started growing boobs before pretty much anyone I knew. I know that this is supposed to be a good thing. These wobbly mounds of flesh are supposed to be attractive and womanly and sexy and all those wonderful things. Only, I was just a kid, like eleven, and none of those things mattered to me at all. What mattered to me is that I suddenly looked funny in a T-shirt and that boys were looking at my chest instead of my face and I was embarrassed to change for gym class. The worst part is that it took my mom forever to notice, and when she did, her solution to the problem wasn't much help.

I made it very clear that I was not interested in bra shopping with my mother. It seemed to me that bras were like underwear or socks, the kind of thing your mother should buy for you when you are somewhere else. My mother did not agree and insisted that I come with her. I discovered another new fact about growing up...there is nothing more embarrassing in the history of the world than being in the lingerie department with your mommy and having someone you know from school walk in.

I can still picture it in every mortifying detail. My mom took a very small white bra off the rack and held it up to my chest while I closed my eyes and tried to will myself into another dimension. Not just a small bra. A *Training Bra*. What exactly were we supposed to be training them to do? Since I didn't even want them, I didn't see why I had to spend time training them!

I opened my eyes and there they were. Tony Giardino and Cody Bellefontaine, the two cutest guys in my class. Just standing there while my mom tried to figure out if my boobs were going to fit into my teeny tiny white cupless bra. Well, they weren't exactly standing in the bra department. They were over by the CD racks in the next aisle but they could definitely see me and I could see them. I was sure they were looking at me and I think I saw Cody gesture in my direction. I pushed my mother away, trying to point at the guys without them seeing me.

My mother looked somewhat blankly in the direction that I was pointing. "What are you doing?" she asked calmly.

"What do you mean, what am I doing? Can't you see them?" I yelled, which wasn't really the smartest thing to do under the circumstances. The guys laughed and walked away before my mother actually bothered to focus. By the time she looked, there was no one there but a salesclerk sorting out CD cases. I could feel my cheeks starting to burn along with my eyes. I don't know why I felt like crying. My stupid eyes welled up at the dumbest times. I told them sternly to stop. My mom would think I was being a baby if I cried over underwear.

"See who, Madison?" she asked me, in that very mild tone she always used at times like this. "Do you mean that sales-clerk? I don't think he is very interested in your underwear, honey." She held another bra up to my chest. She was right; the salesclerk didn't even give us a second glance.

"There were two boys from school. Over there by the CDs. They were totally looking at me and my stupid training bra!" I explained, trying not to whine.

"I'm sure they weren't looking at you. They were probably looking at CDs and not interested in what we were doing at all. Don't worry about it. I'm sure it was your imagination." My mom went back to taking bras out of packages and holding them out for all to see. She really didn't get it at all.

My mom has always said that I have an overactive imagination and that it's my father's fault because his head is always in the clouds. Back then, she said I imagined things as so much worse than they really were because I was starting to deal with my adolescent angst. I didn't know that I had angst of any age. Mom said hormones had something to do with it and that I would grow out of it. In the meantime, she said I should try to tame my imagination. Like a dog. Down, boy.

March 23
They weighed me today. I've gained a pound in the last two weeks. It's those stupid protein shakes. At this rate, I'm going to weigh three hundred pounds before they let me out of here. Then they'll have to send me to a fat farm to get rid of it and then they'll send me back here to put it back on. I'll end up spending the rest of my life being told what to eat and when to go to the bathroom.

I can't even exercise when I want to. They control that too. I have it in my special schedule – once a day for one hour with someone standing there telling me what I can and can't do. Look out: Big Redheaded Sister is watching you.

This place is getting to me. It's full of messed-up girls who spend their whole time moaning about their bodies and asking for other people to tell them what to do about their life. I don't fit in with them. I'm in control of my body and my life. I know what I want and I don't need some counselor to tell me how to live. I didn't ask to be here.

Why is it that it's mostly girls in here, anyway? Is there some rule that says girls have to worry more about how they look than boys? I think there is a rule like that. Most of the girls I know think about their looks all the time and talk about their bodies non-stop. I don't see my brother doing that. He eats what he wants and spends about five minutes getting ready in the morning. As far as I know, he doesn't worry about makeup or hair products or whether his jeans make him look fat.

Women are supposed to be thin and beautiful. It's the way of the world. Anybody who watches TV knows this. When you see a chubby girl on TV, she's usually the funny one without a boyfriend. Overweight women who are trying to be amusing seem to only talk about being fat, and people laugh even though we all know they secretly want to be thin. I don't think being chubby is very funny. I think it's sad. Unless you're a guy, that is. If you're a movie guy you can be old, fat, and gross and still be married to some impossibly gorgeously slim young thing. I think the old fat guy should be put on a serious diet or the woman should dump him. That's what would happen if it was the other way around.

Actually, I think I did see a guy here yesterday. It was just for a second and I may have been imagining it. He walked past my room and seemed to be looking at me. I was going to try to sort of like nod at him in a friendly way, or something daring like that, but he moved away too fast. I went to my door to see where he was but he was gone. Oh well, I've never been good at the whole guy thing anyway. I've never been able to coordinate my brain and my mouth long enough in the presence of an interesting male-type creature to actually say anything remotely intelligent or interesting. I tend to stutter and stammer just enough that I end up drooling, which seems to always put an end to any romantic possibilities.

chapter 4

Fast forward. Grade eight. Puberty in full swing. Pimples and hips competing to see who can get the biggest. My friends are all getting taller and I just seem to stop growing. My legs are long enough to reach the ground, I guess. I begin to learn the first lesson of being a short person: Food is no longer your friend.

No really, I'm not kidding. Once your body stops going up, it has nowhere to go but out. I still liked to eat the same old food but I didn't seem to have as many places to put it, so it made new places. Mostly it landed on my hips and thighs. I knew I wasn't the only one this was happening to, but it felt like it sometimes. Annie sure didn't seem to be changing much.

I didn't really worry about it until my thirteenth birthday. I mean, I knew my body was changing and everything, but at the risk of sounding like my mother, I also knew it was kind of normal. Everyone has to grow up, right? We all do it in different ways, right? I didn't always have to like it but it wasn't as if I was sick or deformed or anything. So I was understandably pissed when my mother informed me that I had to go to the doctor for a checkup. I didn't think I needed to be checked up. I knew that I was in one piece, nothing seemed to be growing where it shouldn't be and even if I wasn't always thrilled with where it ended up, I was feeling relatively healthy. I frequently felt somewhat nuts, but I knew from health class that feeling crazy was an expected side effect of adolescence. I knew this was true because all of my friends, except the always cool Annie, were having meltdowns every couple of weeks or so about all kinds of truly insignificant things that seemed desperately significant when we were thirteen.

"Mom! I don't need the doctor if I'm not sick!"

"You've had regular checkups since you were little. That doesn't change. If anything, it's more important now."

"Why? I have been going to him since I was a baby. I don't need to see him anymore. What's he going to tell me? That I'm not sick. Quite the newsflash."

"Don't use that tone with me. I already made the appointment and you are going."

"You made the appointment without asking me? Half the time you tell me how grown up I am and then you treat me like a little kid. Nice, Mom." I flounced out of the room before she could comment on my tone again. Mom seemed to be commenting on my tone a lot in those days. I didn't know what she was talking about, because I was using the same tone I had always used. She was the one who was using a tone. She was talking to me like I was three years old half the time and like I was thirty-three the other half. I never knew what she wanted from me and everything I said was wrong. I couldn't win with her at all and apparently couldn't even make my own decisions about something as private as a doctor's appointment. I was not impressed but I didn't really have the guts to out and out refuse to go. So I went under protest. My mother noted the protest but was unmoved by it.

Have you ever had one of those full physical things? If you haven't, don't bother. If you have, my sympathies. First they make you strip in a little room with an unlocked door where you're afraid someone is going to walk in on you and see you in your naked glory. They give you this ugly blue gown to put on that ties behind your neck and back and flaps open on your bum. I put it on, trying to tie the string as tightly as I could while grabbing at the back, trying to hold it closed.

"Hello there," the doctor said cheerfully as he entered the room. Glad he was having a good time.

"Hi," I muttered. At least, I imagine that's what I said.

"Hop up on the table for me, please."

Hop? How do you hop when you're trying to hold your gown shut? I got up onto the table, but I did not hop. I eased my way up carefully, looking like a total idiot when I ended up sitting on the hand I was using to keep my modesty.

I noticed the shiny pair of silver stirrups attached to the end of the examination table when I walked in. I knew what they were because I watched TV. I was glad that I was still basically a kid and wasn't anywhere near that type of totally embarrassing scene.

It was still embarrassing enough. I won't go into the details, but let's just say that more skin got exposed than I was planning on showing anyone for a while, let alone a wrinkly old man who didn't seem too worried that he had totally invaded my personal space and blown it away. The whole thing was uncomfortable on a number of levels and so totally unnecessary that I swore it would be the last time I went to a doctor unless I was sure I was dying of something dramatic. I also swore at my mother a few times under my breath for making me come here in the first place.

"So, that's it. You can get dressed. I'll be back in a minute or so to talk with you a little." He smiled at me in that aren't-you-a-good-little-three-year-old way adults use and left the room. I got dressed at the speed of light but was still buttoning up my shirt when he came barreling back into the room without so much as a tap on the door.

"So, you're generally pretty healthy," he started, looking at a file folder as if it held the mysteries of the universe. "Now, about all I need to tell you is that you might want to start thinking about watching your eating habits. A girl your age doesn't want to be adding any unwanted weight." He closed the folder and looked at me as if expecting some brilliant response. I could only stare. Unwanted weight? Did he think I had unwanted weight?

What was he talking about? I mean, I knew that the old hips and thighs were a little bigger than before, but Mom said that was normal. Of course, she said everything was normal. Had she lied? Did she send me to the doctor because she thought I was heading for a weight problem?

"Don't worry. It's not a big deal. You just need to be more careful about what you put in your mouth now that you're menstruating and your growth has slowed down significantly. Now, stop by the desk on the way out and the nurse will give you a nutrition fact sheet that should help you." He smiled at me again, as if he had given me good news, and then left me alone to wander out of his office. I found myself thinking about dragons and wished that there was one in the waiting room who enjoyed doctors for lunch. I didn't stop at the nurse's desk for the nutrition sheet. I didn't want her to know that the doctor thought I was fat. I didn't want my mother to see me with the sheet that confirmed her suspicion I was gaining unwanted weight.

When I got home, I stood in front of the mirror. I looked at myself from the front and the side and used a hand mirror to look at the back. I could definitely see that I wasn't exactly skin and bones, but I didn't really think I looked fat. Maybe the doctor didn't mean anything. Then again, why would he even mention weight if he didn't think it was worth thinking about? I looked again. Well, maybe my butt bulged out a little more than it should. Maybe I should try to lose a pound or two.

It didn't seem like that big a deal. Just cut out snacks. That didn't sound hard.

So, I wasn't too uptight about the whole weight thing at first. After all, none of my friends had ever said I was fat. No one had ever run screaming in horror when they saw me walking down the street. It wasn't a big deal.

Besides, I had much bigger things on my mind. Annie and I were about to enter the hallowed halls of high school. We were a mess of mixed emotions. No, that's not true. I was a mess of mixed emotions. Annie was, of course, cool. I was running around like a hyperactive puppy chasing its tail while Annie sat comfortably and laughed at me.

"What are you doing?" she asked me one day as I frantically emptied out my entire closet, trying on one outfit after another.

"I am trying to find the perfect first-day outfit, of course!" I said, my voice disappearing into the sweater I was trying to pull down over my head while pulling on a pair of pants at the same time. I stood in front of the mirror and tried to see myself from all sides. I looked disgusting and made a sound that matched my looks.

"That's very ladylike of you." Annie shook her head. "Stop staring at yourself in the mirror. It's getting to be a very weird habit. You look fine in that, just like you looked fine in the last ten outfits you tried on. It's just school. You need to relax."

Grinning widely, she smacked me in the face with a pillow. In my mind, it was the dragon pillow, but I'm not sure of that anymore. Anyway, I couldn't let her get away with such violence and I quickly responded with a volley up the back of her head. That started a full-fledged war. Everything was a weapon, including all of the clothes I had thrown on the floor. Stuffed dragons finally took flight, soaring through the air, hitting everything in the room but Annie and me. We totally trashed my room and fell backwards on my bed, laughing at the ceiling.

"You aren't scared at all?" I asked her when I could breathe again.

"No, not really. What exactly are you scared of?" She looked at me sideways, her long black hair half covering her face and spread all over the pillow in a million directions.

I thought about her question for a minute. What was I

scared of? A better question would have been, what wasn't I scared of? I was scared that I wouldn't have good enough marks to get into university some day. I was scared that the teachers would be scarier than the dragon lady in kindergarten and that they would expect me to already know everything. I was scared that I would have ten hours of homework every day. I was scared that I wouldn't fit in with the high school kids. I was scared that there would be boys there and they wouldn't notice me. I was scared that there would be boys there and they would notice me. I was scared that my clothes wouldn't be right, or my hair wouldn't be right, or my backpack wouldn't be right, or my shoes wouldn't be right, or my face wouldn't be right, or my body wouldn't be right – or I wouldn't be right.

"Oh, I don't really know," I said out loud, closing my eyes so that Annie wouldn't be able to see the truth. It wasn't really a full-out lie anyway. I really didn't know how to answer. There were too many choices to pin it down! She probably saw it anyway. Annie could always figure me out even when I didn't want her to. It was like she was psychic. Maybe she was some kind of a seer, like those women we read about in all the dragon books we used to obsess about. Maybe I should have asked her to see into my future and let me know if I was actually going to survive this whole growing up thing at all.

April 1
April Fools' Day. My parents are coming to see me today. Kind of fits, doesn't it? We all feel like fools when we sit there politely with nothing to say. I don't want to talk to them. They took my friends away from me and told me it was for my own

good. Ha. They put me in here and they won't take me back out. I don't have anything to say to them. But if I refuse to see them, it'll get everyone all excited and I'll have to go to the psycho doctor for an extra counseling session. She drives me crazy, sitting there trying to look all understanding when she never says anything that shows she understands a single thing about me. Maybe she does it to keep up business for herself. She would probably be just thrilled if I refused to go see Mommy and Daddy and they could decide I have some sort of parent-hating disorder on top of everything else they've diagnosed me with. Maybe they'll decide that I'm a sociopath with violent tendencies who hates her parents.

Do I hate my parents? I'm PO'd for sure. They will not listen to me at all. They want me to admit to my "problem" and start eating crap and then I would be able to come home and live happily, and fattily, ever after.

Sometimes, though, I kind of wish I could do it for them. They seem so sad when they come. I hate that they're sad. I mean, they deserve to feel guilty for putting me in here but I never wanted anyone to be sad.

I don't hate them. I hate the doctors who persuaded them that I have some big disease.

I didn't make them sad. The doctors made them sad.

Maybe the doctors can visit with my parents instead of me.

I wish I were a sociopath. Then I could make the doctors pay for their sins.

chapter 5

We did manage to start high school and even survived grade nine. I discovered that some of the stuff I had been scared about wasn't so scary after all. I also discovered that some of the stuff was scarier than I had imagined it was going to be. The teachers weren't as bad as I expected. The work wasn't terrible but it wasn't easy either. I worked pretty hard and I had lots of homework. Maybe not ten hours a night, but I still kept pretty busy.

The kids were definitely the scariest part. I couldn't totally figure out who was who at first. Annie and I came from a really small public school and we didn't know all that many kids who went to the high school downtown, which was enormous and had kids in it from all over the city. Oh, in case I am coming off too pathetic here, let me state for the record that Annie was not my only friend. She was just my best friend. I wasn't exactly a social butterfly either but I did have a few people around who seemed to enjoy my company. They weren't what you would call cool. As shocking as it might sound, I was never fully accepted into the cool crowd. This caused me the occasional moment of angst. Annie was somewhat uncool too, but she was also unconcerned. I, however, wondered at times, many times, what it would be like to be popular.

I have made something of a study of this whole popularity thing, and even now I don't really understand what it is that makes someone cool, other than being accepted by the cool crowd, that is. I mean, who decides what cool is in the first place? Someone has to be the first cool person, the one who sets the standards for other cool people. But where does that person come from and how does he or she become cool? Is it a chicken and egg thing – which came first, the person or the cool? Do they just wake up one morning and hear a voice from somewhere in the heavens telling them to embark upon their journey of cool? In all those teen movies, most of the so-called cool types are not exactly nice. They always seem to be incredibly rich and do all kinds of nasty things to the poor uncool people – and to each other. You'd think they'd be happy, but they always look annoyed. Anyway, the movies I found really amazing were the ones in which some poor geeky person becomes cool by taking off their glasses, putting on lots of makeup and wearing tight clothes. It sends a really nice message, doesn't it? All you have to do to be accepted is completely change everything about how you look.

In my school, the so-called cool kids tended to be a little snobby, but I'd never seen anyone do anything particularly terrible to anyone else like in the movies. Anyway, being uncool in our school didn't seem to be the big agony that it is in movies. Hey, I wonder who decided to use the word "cool" in the first place? Cool means "neither warm nor very cold" – just kind of somewhere in between. Maybe cool people are just wishy-washy, mediocre people who don't know how they feel. Something to think about.

What was I talking about? Oh, yeah. Friends who aren't Annie. Well, there's Ruth Edelstein, who's smart and funny and lives with her mom on this weird little farm just heading out of the city. There's Alyssa Petroni, who's into art and music and even managed to get Annie and me into the band. We both played clarinet and neither of us played it very well, but we had fun. And of course there's Devon, who is a total jock woman, extremely tall and extremely strong. She tried to get me to try out for a couple of teams but stopped after I went to a volleyball tryout with her and tripped her twice and knocked her down three times. I decided to stick with solo sports like riding my bike and...well, riding my bike. Devon runs like the wind and always talked about running in the Olympics some day. I told her I'd make the sacrifice of helping her train in a nice warm climate somewhere, but she turned me down. I don't know why. I think I'd be a great coach.

That's about it for people I liked, and who liked me, enough to actually put in this so-called story of my life. Five of us. We hung out together at lunch and sometimes got together at one of our houses for a DVD or something. Our part of the city doesn't have a movie theater or a video arcade or a bowling alley or a swimming pool or a McDonald's or anything much at all, so it took effort and a city bus to do anything more exciting than watch TV.

One of the most exciting things I remember from grade

nine is when Annie and I got invited to Nancy Gerig's chalet for the weekend. We were pretty pumped about the whole thing, because Nancy was super rich, which made her instantly somewhat cool – although she wasn't one of the totally cool – and she had the world's cutest older brother. Actually, I should say that I was excited. Annie thought it sounded like fun but didn't seem as impressed as I was.

I was very impressed. Everyone we knew wanted an invite to the famous chalet of the über-rich Gerig family. I had never even seen a chalet up close and personal. I wasn't actually sure what a chalet was and why it was more exciting than a plain old cottage, but I didn't really care. It sounded wonderful and exotic and I couldn't believe she had actually picked us.

"Maddie, it's not like the president has invited us to the White House. She's just a kid like us," Annie understated one day.

"She is not just a kid. She is one of the cool kids. Well, not exactly one of the cool kids, but she hangs out with them sometimes and they think she's OK because she has all this money and stuff which makes her almost a cool kid and she actually invited us to her chalet and we're not cool at all!" I babbled back at her brilliantly.

"Speak for yourself. I think we're cool enough...although you sound like you're getting a little heated up at the moment!" Annie laughed at her own not-very-funny joke and shook her head.

"Oh my God, I look like I'm wearing a tent!" I whined pathetically. I had a dress on, which is something I didn't wear too often, but I thought it suited the importance of the occasion. I didn't have a lot of pretty clothes, and I figured that people who owned a fancy chalet would expect me to bring something nicer to wear than my usual shorts and T-shirts. I had thought it was wonderful when I first bought it. It was a nice shade of sky blue that the saleslady had assured me matched my eyes and it had short sleeves and was kind of tight around my chest but then sort of floated out around my body. The salesclerk had also told me that it was a very flattering style for me. Maybe because it was supposed to hide most of me from view. Obviously they used magic mirrors in the store that made you look better than you looked in the real world so that they could sell more clothes to unsuspecting schmucks like me. When I looked at myself in the store I hadn't looked like something you would camp in.

"You look fine. The color is nice on you," Annie looked at me and shrugged her shoulders as she turned the page in the magazine she was reading. She had the same old jean shorts and T-shirt on that she'd had for about three years and it didn't seem to bother her at all.

"I'm not talking about the color. I'm talking about how fat it makes me look! I can't believe this! I can't wear this! What if her brother is there? He'll think there are two of me! Now I have nothing but my crappy old shorts which probably look even worse on me!"

"What are you talking about? You don't look fat. You look like you have a pretty dress on. If you really want to look sexy, you should try wearing one of these!"

She laughed and handed me the page she was looking at. The model was ultra thin and totally beautiful, every rib standing out clearly underneath the two little triangles that called themselves a bathing suit top. More bones stuck out just above the slightly larger triangle that was pretending to be a bathing suit bottom. She was standing on the deck of a sailboat, pretending to steer it and looking very pleased with herself. I thought of my own bathing suit, a one-piece wonder in black. I bought it because someone told me that black was slimming. I hadn't thought anything of it at the time, but now I started wondering why anyone thought I needed slimming or that I needed a flattering dress. I knew that I didn't look anything like that model when I had my bathing suit on. Most of my bones were pretty well buried and I didn't think anyone would call me sexy.

Annie snagged the magazine back, still smiling.

"Isn't that pathetic? As if she actually knows how to sail a boat. Besides, she's so thin she'd probably blow away if a decent wind came up! Anyway, kid, I've got to go. I have to do my ten minutes of packing. See you tomorrow!"

I didn't sleep well that night, between the excitement and the worry. I couldn't stop agonizing about how I looked in my dress or my bathing suit, or my skin for that matter, and whether or not Nancy's brother was going to be there. Not that I thought he would notice me anyway, but I didn't want him to think bad stuff about me. I don't remember the next day's drive up to the chalet very well. I was probably half asleep.

Boys were very confusing back then. I wanted them to notice me but I could never think of anything to say to them when they did. I kind of wanted a boyfriend but I had no idea what I would do with one if I found him. I wanted boys to think

I was pretty, but I didn't really want to know what they thought just in case they thought I was an ugly pig. When I thought about boys, it was kind of like my mind turned into a blender where I put all of these weird thoughts and feelings that swirled around totally out of control.

I do remember my first look at the chalet. It's like a snapshot in my mind, clear and well developed. It was pretty amazing. It was made from logs and was incredibly tall with two levels of balconies on the outside overlooking the ski hills. Inside was even more incredible. There were balconies on the inside as well, surrounding a huge stone fireplace that reached all the way to the ceiling. The furniture was all made of heavy wood and had colorful cushions that looked soft and comfy.

Nancy's brother was there, but he wasn't particularly interested in his sister's little friends. That was fine by me. At least, I thought it was fine, but at the same time I couldn't help but wonder why he wasn't interested. As I said, totally out of control! Anyway, there was lots to do there, between the boats and the swimming and the walking trails, and we had fun, which took my mind off all my messed-up thoughts, and we were all starving when we came in for supper. Nancy's mom had made a delicious meal and we all dug in. Once we had finished the barbecued hamburgers and potato salad, Nancy's mom brought out this absolutely amazing-looking chocolate cake. Man, did I want a piece of that cake! But as she brought it to the table, I had a sudden flash of the sight of the oversized blue tent in the mirror.

"No thanks," I said politely, as a piece was passed my way.

I peeked over at Annie to see if she had noticed, but she was already digging into hers so she was distracted by the chocolate. Mrs. Gerig looked surprised.

"Oh, dear. Don't you like chocolate cake?" she asked, in the same tone she might have used to ask me if I liked breathing.

"Oh, yes. It looks delicious. But I'm trying to cut down," I said, trying not to look at my hips when I said it.

"Well, then, good for you! I wish I had your willpower!" Mrs. Gerig beamed at me and then looked around the table to make sure everyone had been served before she proceeded to down a giant piece of the calorie fest along with everyone else...everyone else but me.

As I lay in the totally comfortable bunk bed that night below Annie and thought about the day, I didn't think of the fun we had. All I could think about was Mrs. Gerig's comment. Why did she think it was good for me to cut out dessert? Did she think I was fat, too? But then again, she had also complimented me. It was nice to have someone wish they were more like me. Restless and unable to sleep, I snuck out of bed and tiptoed to the bathroom down the hall.

I closed the door quietly and turned on the light. The bathroom had only a toilet and a small cabinet with an even smaller mirror over top. I could only see my face in the mirror, which wasn't what I wanted. I climbed awkwardly onto the edge of the cabinet, praying that I wouldn't break it, and balanced on my knees, trying to see my body. All I managed to do was fall off the cabinet and make a big noise, so I gave up and went to bed.

"What happened?" Annie asked in a sleepy voice. "I thought I heard a crash."

"Oh, I just dropped something. It's OK. Go back to sleep." I lay down and closed my eyes, wondering why I had just lied to my very best friend.

April 4

I saw him again. Just for a second or two, but it was definitely him. He has that white blond hair some people have, kind of curly. I couldn't see much else but he seemed kind of cute from a distance. He walked right past my door and stopped on the other side of the hall, looking in here. I even got up and went over to make an effort talk to him but he was gone before I got there. He must be a patient. Visitors don't come to this part of the building. We have to go downstairs and see them in this nice little room where everything is so pleasant and perfect that you would think we were at some upscale university instead of a pseudo-guesthouse for messed-up dieters.

I didn't really think that guys did the whole anorexia/bulimia thing. But I'm pretty sure everyone is here for the same reason. Oh, that's what they call it, by the way. Anorexia nervosa. Supposedly I have it. Sounds like an Italian opera singer. I can't even sing! We learned about it in health class, and I read about it on the Internet back in the good old days when I could still communicate with the outside world. Half the celebrities out there supposedly have it too. I can't believe they think I have some looney-tune disease just because I don't want to be fat! I am not starving myself. I don't have some big emotional issue here. But try telling that to the dumb-ass doctors and so-called counselors. Now they've decided I have "bulimic" tendencies too because I got rid of the stupid protein shake and was dumb enough to get caught. They think there's something wrong with getting rid of something that's going to harm your body. They think I'm self-destructive. I think it's practical. I think it means I care about my body. I think I'm self-*constructive*.

I wonder if he'll talk to me?

chapter 6

After the chalet trip I got kind of into the whole routine of cutting out food and showing off my willpower. I got used to going without desserts and snacks pretty quickly, and I liked the way it felt. I started reading about diets in magazines. It wasn't hard to find information. Every single magazine in existence that had a female on the cover seemed to headline fifteen different ways to lose ten pounds. There was an ad on every second page that made great promises to help anyone lose any amount of weight they wanted to. Pop-up ads invaded the Internet every few seconds advertising all of the same things. You could definitely tell that the people in the "after" pictures were a lot happier than the fat slobs in the "before" pictures.

I started cutting out other stuff and counting calories. My family didn't really seem to notice much so I kept on doing it. Breakfast and lunch were always fly-by meals and supper was a family deal where everyone was always talking and serving themselves. No one paid much attention to what anyone else was eating. My parents were pretty into the whole good nutrition bit, and there wasn't too much junk food floating around our house anyway, so it wasn't really all that hard to cut back. By the summer I could tell that something was changing. My clothes seemed a little looser, and I had to buy a belt to hold up the jean shorts that had fit me the year before. It was kind of a cool feeling, and I started trying to figure out ways to lose more weight faster.

Annie and I didn't usually spend the summers together. She had this big family cottage out west and all of her relatives spent most of the summer there. It's kind of interesting, actually. Annie's great-great-grandparents on her dad's side came here from Japan and settled on the west coast years and years ago. During the Second World War, her great-grandparents and two of her grandparents were put in one of those internment camps. I never knew about it until we were studying it in history and Annie told me the story. It made it all so real and so sad. Her grandmother came to school one time when she was here on a visit and talked to the class. She didn't really remember much because she was so little when she was there, but she had some of her family's memories mixed in with her own and the stories were amazing. I couldn't believe how strong they all were and how they went on with their lives and kept on building their family in this country after all that happened.

My family is pretty small so I could never really understand how Annie could stand spending the whole summer out at some cottage with no phone or TV or any of the other essentials, like a computer. I have my mom and dad and Steve. That's pretty much it. My mom's parents live about a five-hour drive away. We see them on holidays and stuff but don't visit all that much. A weekend here or there. I can't tell for sure, but I don't think my mom and my grandma are exactly close. They're polite to each other and everything but they seem kind of tense when they're together. My grandpa is pretty quiet and seems almost shy. Steve and I have always really liked being with him when we do visit. He's just kind of gentle. Grandma can be a lot louder and likes to tell us what to do even though she hardly sees us. My mom gets annoyed with her and then she tells my mother what to do. That doesn't tend to go over very well. My dad's parents both passed away. His dad died when he was just a little kid and his mom died when I was little. Sad. I have an uncle on my dad's side who has a couple kids. I've only met them a few times. They seem pretty nice but I don't really feel like they are family or anything. Polite strangers, mostly. My mom has a sister who doesn't have any kids.

I have Steve. There seems to be a two-kid pattern here. He's kind of a typical big brother. He can be a total pain in the backside when he wants to be, the champion of teasing and making my life miserable, and then he can turn around and be totally nice and supportive when I need someone to help me or protect me from things that go bump in the night. Nice when he needs to be and a total pain when he wants to be. I kind of hope he has some kids some day in the distant future so I have nieces and nephews. It might be fun to have a bigger family someday. I don't know if I'll ever have kids. So far, the whole romance department is pretty lacking.

Annie has more relatives than I can count. She said there are always lots of cousins around in the summer and they really liked spending time together, swimming and hiking and doing other activities that she seemed excited about but seemed less than thrilling to me, unless of course they came with a weekend at a cool chalet. I try to imagine being surrounded by piles of people who are all related to me, doing all sorts of outdoorsy things, but it just doesn't compute for me at all.

Then again, Annie thought that my summer plans were pretty boring too, only she was always too polite to actually say so. I usually spend part of my summer hanging around doing nothing in particular except practicing the piano and trying to stay out of my mother's way so she won't find things for me to do. Sometimes I go out to Ruth's place and try out farm life for a day or two. She has a couple of horses that she spends lots of time with in the summer, and she has tried to teach me to ride a few times. I decided I was better on a bike. My bike listens to me and doesn't have teeth. Alyssa does a lot of traveling in the summer. She still has lots of relatives in Europe that her mom takes her to see. I offered to go and keep her company a couple of times, but no one took me up on it. Devon did the sports camp thing most years when she was little, and she's now training to be a counselor so she can actually make some money. So, amusing myself in the summer has always been a challenge, except when I went to camp.

Yes, I said camp. I know that sounds kind of weird from someone who just dismissed the idea of hanging out at a cottage swimming and hiking, but my camp wasn't exactly what you think of when you talk about camp. My dad always called camp my home away from home, only better. It was pretty nice. We slept in cabins with actual mattresses on the beds. There was a lounge for older campers where you could watch TV at night and even a computer that you could go on if you signed up for some time. The food was totally awesome. Everyone pigged out the whole time they were there. The older campers, like me, pretty much did whatever they wanted. We could swim and hike if we wanted to. We could also just hang out and do nothing in particular if we wanted to. That's what we usually chose. My mom and dad would have completely freaked if they had known that their hard-earned cash was being spent on me finding a different place to hang out, doing the same stuff I did at home. I'm pretty sure they thought I was learning all about survival training and knot tying and other terribly important life skills.

There was a group of girls who went to camp with me most years. We had known each other since we were about ten and always managed to book the same three weeks even though we never actually talked to each other during the year. We were summer friends, I guess.

I had expected that summer after grade nine to be the same as any other. I figured my summer friends would all be there just like every other year and that I'd have a great time and come home to my real life.

It didn't work out that way. Somehow, the girls I usually spent the summer with ended up at camp during a different session than me and I ended up standing in a strange cabin surrounded by even stranger girls. I could feel that sick feeling in my stomach that I always get when something goes wrong and I can't do anything to fix it. Kind of like how I felt right after my kindergarten teacher found the worms, only worse. The girls strutting around the cabin were not only strangers to me, they were obviously friends to each other. They didn't even look at me. They just picked their bunks and pinned up pictures of their perfect-looking boyfriends. They all seemed to be wearing designer clothes that fit them like they were made for them. They looked sophisticated and sure of themselves, everything I wasn't. I felt like a drab little caterpillar in a room full of high-class butterflies. Every one of those girls weighed about three pounds and most of that was perfect, shimmering hair in every lustrous shade that you've ever seen on TV.

I never mentioned my hair, did I? That's because it really isn't worth mentioning most of the time. I have curly brown hair. Annie calls me a brunette, which sounds nice, but my hair is really just plain old brown, kind of like garden soil. Earthy, I guess. Some people tell me that curly hair is a good thing. My mom keeps reminding me that people spend a lot of money trying to get their hair as curly as mine. It was nice of her to say so, but it wasn't really true. When you get your hair permed, the curls are all perfect and stay just right all of the time. When you have naturally curly hair, the curls do whatever they want to do, whenever they want to do it. My hair was more often frizz than curl, and I tried everything I could to get it to go straight. Everything I tried worked for about three minutes, and then my hair pouffed right back up.

Anyway, back to the summer of the alien invasion. The first few days were basically awful. I didn't think I was going to survive the three weeks but I didn't want to give in and call home like some kind of baby-faced first-year camper. I wandered around by myself most of the time, avoiding the other girls as much as I could. The only time I had to be with them was at meals and at night. Nighttime was the worst because they all stayed up half the night talking to each other and pretending I wasn't there, while I put my dragon pillow over my face and pretended I wasn't there.

Mealtimes were pretty bad also. I could see all of them staring at me, judging everything I put in my mouth and wondering how someone like me could eat at all. So, I started playing a game with myself. I would look at all the food and figure out what had the least calories. I had bought myself one of those little calorie-counter books before I came to camp. You know the kind. They're these little pocketbook things with lists of food items inside and the number of calories in each one. It was pretty interesting reading. I was shocked at some of the junk I'd been eating. No wonder the doctor of doom had told me to watch it. Anyway, I had tried to memorize as many of the everyday type foods as I could, like one slice of white bread has 110 calories. So I would look at the table full of food and try to eat as few calories as I could without going totally hungry. It was kind of fun in a way, because it was my game and no one knew anything about it. Well, not at first, anyway.

About four days into that first week of horror, someone actually spoke to me.

"You don't eat much, do you?" she asked, looking at my plate. It was hamburger night, and the table was covered with plates of burgers and fries. I had some lettuce and tomato slices on my plate and one hamburger patty without the bun. I wasn't sure about the hamburger's calorie content so I was only eating half. I was so startled to be noticed that at first I didn't say anything.

"You can talk, can't you?" Someone else was talking to me. That was more conversation than I had had all week. I wasn't sure if I could remember how to talk.

"Of course I can talk!" I said, brilliantly.

"So, what's with the rabbit food?" someone else asked. I looked up to find six pairs of perfectly made-up eyes on me and my plate. I didn't know what to say. They already thought I was a total loser. Maybe I should tell them I had an ulcer or something. Right. That would make me popular. Tell everyone I have a middle-aged man's disease.

Would I make matters any worse by telling the truth? Could matters be any worse?

"I'm, well, just, um, trying to, you know, cut down." I nodded at my own wisdom, looking at my plate as if it held the answers to all of the great questions of life. Wilted lettuce and faded tomato slices stared back at me silently. No answers there.

"Cool. I'm Keisha by the way." I looked up, stunned. She actually sounded sincere. She smiled at me. I smiled back.

"Maddie," I said.

"So, are you on a diet?" Keisha asked. The other girls looked interested. I thought about her question for a second before answering. I hadn't really thought about it in that exact way before. Was I on a diet? Did that make me sound cooler or more like a loser? I thought of all of the magazines and how excited they seemed to be when someone famous went on a diet.

"Yeah, I guess so," I answered, my powers of conversation obviously fascinating all of them.

"Good for you," one of the other girls sighed. (I later learned her name was Savannah.) "I keep on trying to start one but it's just so hard." She patted her completely flat stomach and sighed again.

"Oh, I know. It's, like, you want to lose weight but you just can't give up the food. One day, I'm going to look like my mother and then I'll just want to die!" Keisha put her hand to her chest dramatically. Everyone laughed, including me, even though I thought it was a little rude talking about your mother that way.

And that was it. For the rest of camp, I kind of belonged. I didn't really have much in common with them, but we talked about food a lot and they all read my calorie-counter book with me. A couple of them even tried keeping track for a couple of days. They showed me how to do my makeup and Savannah managed to straighten my hair and keep it that way for more than three minutes. Annie wouldn't have recognized me with my blue eye shadow and flowing locks! Devon would have split a gut laughing, but Alyssa would have totally approved. I would have fit right in with the beautiful people in Europe.

I found it easier and easier to keep track of the calories. Everyone seemed so impressed with me, that I was determined to do an even better job of the whole diet thing for the rest of camp. It was kind of hungry going at first, but I got used to it. By the middle of camp, I was down to less than nine hundred calories a day. Not bad at all.

Parents' Day was always about halfway through the session. Not everyone had parents show up, but mine always did. Even though I was at the relatively grown-up age of almost fifteen, they arrived on cue that year as well. They always sprang me from camp for the afternoon and took me to a nearby motel where we ate real restaurant food and swam in the chlorinated pool.

"So, what will it be first, food or chlorine?" my dad asked when I climbed into the car.

"Oh, we already had lunch, so I'm not hungry. I'd like a swim, though." I looked out the window as I answered. We hadn't really had lunch and I was actually hungry, but I couldn't face the whole lunch-at-a-restaurant routine. My dad always figured that the camp starved us and he insisted on ordering chocolate milkshakes and cheeseburgers. There was no way I was going to risk eating that much food all at once. The milkshake alone would blow the calorie count for the day.

I changed quickly into my black "slimming" suit when we got to our room. Like all hotel rooms, this one seemed to have a mirror on every wall and I stopped for a minute to look at myself when I came out of the bathroom. The suit definitely looked different. The straps kept coming down off my shoulders and there was a saggy look to the material that I hadn't noticed before. I stood at the mirror looking at myself from all angles. I put my hand on my belly to see if it was getting smaller. I looked a little closer. Well, maybe it looked a little smaller, but not much. That suit really wasn't all that slimming after all. I still looked pretty chubby. Maybe I should try for eight hundred calories a day.

"What are you doing?" my mother asked. I jumped at the sound of her voice. I hadn't heard her come in through the adjoining door.

"I'm just getting ready to go swimming," I answered, turning away from the mirror and trying to smile cheerfully. I wanted to look at myself again, to see if the rest of me still looked as chubby as my stomach, but I had the feeling my mom wouldn't like that.

"Why were you holding your stomach like that? Are you sick?" Mom moved in, with the "I'm getting a thermometer" look that she always gets when one of us so much as sneezes. She reached out and felt my forehead. I shook my head, knocking her hand off.

"I'm fine. I was just looking at my suit. I think I need a new one."

My mother stood and looked at me, presumably considering the wisdom of buying a new suit. I felt uncomfortable under her gaze. She was staring at me like she had never seen me before.

"You look very thin," she said, taking me by the shoulders and turning me around like some kind of inanimate object.

"I am not thin. I'm just...changing. You know, adolescence and all that. It's normal." I tried not to put too much sarcasm into the last word as I gently took her hands off me so as not to tick her off and went out to the pool. I had the feeling she wasn't convinced but I didn't really care. Mothers always thought something was wrong with you when there wasn't. How could she think I looked thin when I was obviously still overweight? Besides, she was the one who sent me to the doctor in the first place.

The visit wasn't quite as much fun as when I was younger. Part of growing up, I guess.

The rest of camp passed by pretty fast. I worked on keeping up with the other girls while knowing that I would never really measure up. I kept working on my calorie studies and was an expert by the end of the session. I was definitely down to eight hundred, and the girls were all totally amazed at my willpower.

We said goodbye at the end of the summer with all sorts of promises to write and talk and chat online and see each other again.

That was the last time I saw any of them. It wasn't any great loss. I mean, they turned out to be pretty nice and everything, but I knew deep down that I didn't really belong with girls like them. They were the kind of girls who were always standing in the bright lights so that everyone could look at them. I was more the kind of girl who sat back in the shadows a bit so that no one would really notice her.

April 6
"So, I saw you eyeing the Wolfman. You interested?"

I looked up, startled that someone was talking to me. There was a girl leaning against my open door. She was standing with her arms folded, looking quite comfortable and like she had been here for a while. She was wearing all black, sweat pants and a T-shirt that had a red patterned bird of some kind on it, I think an eagle. Her hair was as black as her clothes, cut super short, with sort of spiky bangs. It was straight and shiny, the kind of hair I've always wanted. Her eyes, which were looking at me like I was a nutcase, were almost navy blue. She was not typically pretty like the perfect girls in high school but there was something about her that made you wish you looked exactly like her.

"Hello. Anyone in there?" she asked.

"Hi," I said lamely, showing off my usual top-notch social skills.

"So, are you interested?" she asked.

I had no idea what she was talking about, so I shrugged and said, "Interested in what?"

"The Wolfman. I saw you looking at him earlier, and he's been kind of skulking past your room. Just wondering what's up with that." She came in without an invitation and sat on my bed. I turned in my chair to look at her.

I had worked pretty hard to avoid everyone since I came here and I thought I had made it pretty clear that I wasn't in the market for new buddies. I tried to look unfriendly, which wasn't very hard, but she didn't seem to care. She just sat there looking interested until I felt like I had to say something.

"The Wolfman?" I asked, even though I was pretty sure I knew who she meant. That gorgeous guy was called the Wolfman? I knew this place was some kind of an evil cult. This girl was probably a vampire.

"Well, that's what I call him. He calls himself Wolf, which shouldn't really be his name, 'cause when I first heard that there was some guy here named Wolf I thought he might be someone kind of exciting but when I checked him out I discovered, well, not so much."

"What?" I asked, which didn't really make sense, but nothing she said made sense to me either.

"Well, I thought he might be all cool and dangerous, like

he earned the name from his dark reputation or something. But, unfortunately, it's really just a name he got by accident. I think he's, like, part German or something. His grandfather or uncle or aunt or great-uncle twice removed was named Wolfgang so he got it as a middle name. I guess he liked it better than his first name so he grabbed it. But he seems more like a pussy cat to me than a Wolf, all soft and fluffy."

"What's his first name?" At least the question made sense this time.

"I think it's Pieter or something like that. He never really uses it around here though. I call him Wolfman just to bug him. Otherwise it's Wolf."

"Oh."

"So, you're Madison," she stated matter of factly. I wasn't sure why she knew my name when I had no idea who she was, but I didn't ask. I already looked stupid enough.

"Yeah, but mostly people call me Maddie."

"Cool. I'm Marina. My dad picked it out for me but my mom never liked it because she thinks it sounds like a place where you buy boats, which of course it does, but it's still an OK name. She let my dad have first pick because they thought I was only kid number one, but they got divorced so I ended up being the only kid period. Sucks for them. Anyway, my mom calls me Marie, which is not my name but I answer anyway so as not to piss her off. You can call me Marina."

"Oh," I said because I couldn't think of anything else to say.

"It's actually a Latin word that means 'of the sea.' I like that. I love the ocean. I'm kind of hoping to be a marine biologist some day. We lived right on the ocean when I was little, but I don't really remember back then all that well. Weird, isn't it? I mean, do you think I fell in love with the sea because of my name, or did my dad somehow know I was going to love it when he picked it, or do I love it because I lived near it even though I don't remember it?"

"Um, I don't know."

"I don't expect you to. I was being rhetorical. At least my question was. Where'd you get your name?"

"It's a street in New York. Not sure why my parents named me after a street in New York. Maybe I'll end up studying streets some day." I hoped she caught my sarcasm and decided I wasn't worth talking to. She either didn't catch it or didn't care because she didn't leave.

"So, you want me to introduce you two?" she asked. This time I knew what she was talking about.

"No thanks. I'm not really into getting to know too many people." Which was a lie, because the truth was that I actually wanted to get to know the only guy I'd seen here. At least I thought I did. Marina just kind of laughed.

"You trying to tell me something?" she asked, sounding totally unoffended.

"No," I lied again. What was wrong with me?

"Good, 'cause I need someone fresh to talk to. I'm sick of all these babes with nothing interesting to say. Trust me to come up with a girl's disease. All I have is the Wolfman, and I'm pretty sure he's afraid of me."

"Why?"

"Why is he afraid of me or why do I think he is?"

"Either one."

"Well, every time I talk to him he finds somewhere more interesting to be. He doesn't seem afraid of you, though. I think he's kind of interested. Which won't make you very popular because he's the only guy on our floor and the girls who are still interested in guys have all made their play for him."

"I don't think he's interested in me and I am definitely not interested in guys at the moment. I have enough to worry about." Although I had to admit, at least to myself, that I didn't mind the idea that I could be unpopular because the sole dose of testosterone in this estrogen festival was actually looking at me.

"Yeah, this place can suck big time when you first get here. Well, actually it sucks the whole time you're here but you get used to it after a while."

"How long have you been here?"

"Not long enough to get used to it," she said with a grin. She stood up and stretched a bit in that way people do who are dancers, all graceful and elegant. She looked at me and kind of nodded like I had passed some test.

"I'll see you around, Maddie. Let me know if you change your mind about the Wolfman."

"OK. Bye."

I watched her walk out. She walked like a dancer, sort of on the balls of her feet with a little bounce in every step. I wondered about that name thing. How could her father have known she would want to be a marine biologist? It was more likely that she decided to go that way because of her name. I heard of some professor who studied birds and his last name was Sparrow. Speaking of names, Wolf sure was an interesting one. I never would have guessed that was his name in a million years. I mean, it wasn't really his name but he used it, so I guess it was his name. Kind of funky, actually. Wolf. Not that I was interested. I wasn't. I didn't have time for guys. Or for girls. I wasn't here to make friends. I had friends. Real friends who cared about me and were probably worried sick about me. Friends I was banned from talking to in this hellhole.

All I had time to do was to figure out how I got here and how to get myself back out.

chapter 7

I was always excited to see Annie again after the summer. We always had a million things to talk about. We usually bought each other something new to add to the dragon collection in the summer and would get together the night before school started to exchange gifts and talk about the new year coming up.

When the doorbell rang the night before day one of grade ten, I grabbed the dragon T-shirt I had bought Annie on the way home from camp and ran down the stairs to open the door. I couldn't wait to tell her all about the aliens. I knew she'd have a good laugh over the thought of me in makeup at summer camp.

I opened the door, a big smile on my face. Annie was standing on the porch, a bag in her hand and a smile on her face as well. Her hair was tied back from her face with a red scarf that matched her shirt and she was wearing crazy-looking shorts with huge flowers on them. I was about to make a comment about her outfit when Annie's smile seemed to do an instant flip.

"Oh my God, Maddie, what happened? Are you all right?" She stepped forward and put a hand on my arm. I looked at her as if she'd grown two heads.

"What are you talking about? Of course I'm all right! Am I bleeding or something?" I patted my face, feeling for large gashes that would panic Annie.

"No, it's just you're so thin. You look like you've lost twenty pounds since I last saw you. Have you had the flu or something?" She didn't step back, like anyone else would have done when wondering if I had some dreadful disease, but leaned in to look at me more carefully. That's the kind of friend she was.

"I haven't lost twenty pounds!" I said indignantly, though I admit I was secretly pleased that she might have thought that was possible. "Maybe four or five. I've just been watching what I eat a little. I probably grew a bit too. Come on, we have a lot to talk about." Annie still had her hand on my arm so I just turned around and started walking up the stairs. I didn't want to talk about the whole weight thing with Annie. Even though she was my best friend in the whole world, I didn't really think she would understand. She had never had to worry about her body the way I had. How could she know what it was like?

It was really strange that night. We sat in my room like we always did and talked about the same things we always had. She gave me a beautiful dragon made out of soapstone that I added to the collection on my shelf. I gave her the T-shirt that had two dragons holding hands and the slogan "Dragons Are Forever" on it. She tried it on, and we laughed at how big it was on her. We looked at clothes and talked about school and boys.

Everything seemed the same as it always had been, except that it just wasn't the same. Every once in a while I would catch Annie looking at me with a strange expression on her face as if wondering what I was thinking. I tried to keep my expression and mind blank so she wouldn't use her seer skills and take a walk inside my mind.

I had my first major crush in grade ten. Jesse Grayson. He had his locker about three down from mine. He was definitely part of the cool crowd and way out of my league. I spent most of September dropping books on my foot while trying not to look like I was staring at him. He became my favorite topic of online conversation with Annie when I was supposed to be doing my homework. All of our conversations were probably almost identical, kind of like variations on a single theme, like some of the piano pieces I used to play.

alwaysannie says:
ur just as cool as any of those other girls,
Jesse'd be lucky to have u

madmaddie says:
yeah…guys like Jesse always go out with the band
nerds. lol

alwaysannie says:
nerds cause we spend time hanging out in the music
room listening to music and practicing???

madmaddie says:
i guess in nerd world, the band's the least nerdy.
i guess there's even a couple of the cool kids in

band, computer geeks too. equal opportunity nerd
land.

angelicallyssa says:
hey! Don't knock band land. so not nerdy. coolest
of cool!

alwaysannie says:
hey, isn't JG in band? so he's like a band nerd
too. something in common, right?

madmaddie says:
totally in the band but totally not nerdy!!!
trumpet. so cool. sigh. even in dance band. so
cute!!!! so doesn't know i'm alive. sigh louder.
wish he would notice me.

angelicallyssa says:
u could drop ur clarinet on his foot.

madmaddie says:
lol better than dropping books on mine!

alwaysannie says:
so say hi to him

madmaddie says:
no way. then he would notice me!!

alwaysannie says:
U R CRAZY!!!

angelicallyssa says:
totally!!!!!!!!!!!!!!!!!!!!!!!!!!!!!!!!!!!

madmaddie says:
crazy for him!!!!!!!!!!!!!!!!!!!

alwaysannie says:
then talk to him!!!!!

angelicallyssa says:
sing to him!!!

madmaddie says:
don't want to kill him! anyway, easy for u to say.
y don't u talk to him?

alwaysannie says:
not my type of B/F

madmaddie says:
OMG U R CRAZY!!! he's the cutest

rowdyruth says:
who we talking about?

angelicallyssa says:
JG

rowdyruth says:
JG??

alwaysannie says:
u know. cute, trumpet, cute, guy, cute ☺

rowdyruth says:
oh. yeah. JG. who likes him?

angelicallyssa says:
MM

madmaddie says:
no one.

rowdyruth says:
AA beat u! now i know. he's cute. go for it.

alwaysannie says:
just talk to him. gotta go. math. bfn.

angelicallyssa says:
he won't bite

rowdyruth says:
maybe she wants him to bite. ☺ haha

angelicallyssa says:
lol

madmaddie says:
u ppl are no help. H&K.

angelicallyssa says:
just bugging u. u should just say hi. anyway, gtr.
math too.

madmaddie says:
yeah, me too.

rowdyruth says:
i just got here. sucks. guess i'll find someone
else to talk to. TTFN.

madmaddie says:
off to dream sad lonely dreams. hahaha. ttyl

I got my chance to meet Jesse in the last possible way I had ever thought would happen to me. Suzanne Albright, of the cooler-than-cool crowd, actually approached me one day at lunch. I know that doesn't look all that mind blowing down here in black and white, but trust me, it was. Every school has a Suzanne Albright. She's the one girl that everyone wants to be noticed by, male or female. She's the one with the perfect hair, perfect face, perfect wardrobe hanging on a perfect thin and beautiful body, perfect boyfriend always older and athletic, perfect family with lots of money. She's totally sure of herself and confident that everyone else thinks she is as perfect as she believes herself to be. She's kind of a composite of the whole group of girls from camp. I'm not sure if anyone actually likes her, but everyone wants to be liked by her. Looking back, I'm not sure if the one girl ever actually has a personality or any actual character at all, but back in grade ten I didn't care any more than anyone else did.

Anyway, I honestly can't remember precisely what she said, but I seem to remember something about my outfit looking nice on me. It was everything I could do not to actually swoon at her feet. Suzanne Albright of the wardrobe of many colors actually liked something I had on. I can't remember now exactly what I had on, but it was likely something new and form fitting. I still wasn't thrilled with the form that it was fitting, but it was smaller than the year before and I was a little more willing to show it off. Obviously, thinner was cooler, if Suzanne was any judge. Actually, in my mind, Suzanne was judge, jury, and the guy who drew the pictures in court. So, it was all I could do not to perform a happy dance when she followed the compliment up with an actual invitation to one of her cool crowd parties. A party that was going to have all of the beautiful people at it. A party that was going to have the gorgeous and wonderful Jesse Grayson at it.

I'd like to think that I was suave and smooth and answered with some sort of witty response that would make her think that I was a good choice to join her entourage of minions. I don't actually remember what I said, but I am pretty sure I stammered and stuttered and probably drooled. Always so very cool.

April 10
I saw that guy again. I mean, I saw Wolf again. Or Pieter or whoever he is. He just kind of walked by my room and sort of looked in my direction. I think I opened my mouth to say something brilliant but he was gone by the time my brain realized that my mouth was trying to speak. Maybe they have therapy for girls who can't talk to boys. I should check it out. I could just spend my whole day floating from one therapist to the other until my mind is completely out of my control.

Am I still technically a girl or am I officially a woman now? I can't drink legally until I'm nineteen but I've been able to drive since I was sixteen. I can't vote until next year. Why is it that the government thinks that a sixteen-year-old can operate a two-ton piece of fast-moving machinery but they can't walk into a little portable closet and put a checkmark in a box?

Anyway, I am probably not an adult yet as far as anyone official cares. How old do I have to be to check myself out of here? I bet none of these guard dogs around here would tell me if I asked them. My parents sure wouldn't tell me. Maybe that guy would know. Of course, to find out, I would have to be able to actually put enough words together to ask him. I bet Marina never has trouble figuring out what to say to guys...or anyone else for that matter. I wonder how someone like her ended up in a place like this? Does she have friends somewhere who are missing her? She seems like the kind of person who would have friends.

Of all of the things I hate about this place, the thing I hate the most is that I don't have the Internet. I have a laptop because they think that I need to write and they don't want me to have a pencil or a pen in case I decide to off myself with it – that would just be gross by the way – but they have decided that the World Wide Web is some sort of evil network designed to negatively influence impressionable people like me. That isn't exactly how they put it, but it's close enough. They have no idea how much I miss the Internet. I would feel a whole lot saner if I had it here.

Did I mention that this joint is called "Living for Life"? Can you think of a dorkier name on the face of the planet? It sounds like some sort of whacked-out religious cult that's going to launder my brain with their bull until it's squeaky clean. More evidence that this *is* a cult. Maybe some door-to-door salesman showed up at my parents' house and sold them a year's subscription to hell on earth.

How can they take away all of my rights and freedoms and then try to tell me how to live for life? I don't have any life at the moment. No phone, no TV, no Internet, no friends, no nothing!

No friends. How pathetic is that. Maybe they can add that to the list of things wrong with me and make me have extra therapy sessions to discuss my lack of social skills and apparent inability to communicate effectively with my peers. Gag me.

Actually, I do have friends. Real, true friends who care about me and accept me just the way I am and aren't trying to change me and tell me to do things differently. I'm just not allowed to talk to them. I miss them so much I feel like I'm going mental. All I need is half an hour a day on the computer and I'll be OK. All I need is some time to talk to my girls.

We were a team and now I'm not there and no one even knows where I am. It's so unfair. The only people who understand me at all are hidden away from me now, floating somewhere out in cyber space while I rot away in this supposedly "real" world. They probably look for me every night and wonder why I'm not online. I didn't even get a chance to say goodbye to them before I got tossed in here.

I feel like screaming.

chapter 8

alwaysannie says:
u talking to SA???

madmaddie says:
totally! can u believe it? man, SA talking to me!
little old me. well, not exactly little but still
me. she liked my clothes and told me she liked
them. amazing! i might have to retire the outfit or
something, you know like a sports jersey. what did
i have on anyway?

alwaysannie says:
u sound a little nuts, MM. is that all she said?

madmaddie says:
is that all she said? r u nuts? this is
amazingness of all amazingness!

alwaysannie says:
so what did she say?

madmaddie says:
i can't remember. Lol

alwaysannie says:
don't believe you!

madmaddie says:
invited me to one of her friday parties. this
friday. she listed a bunch of people who were
coming and…guess who??????

angelicallyssa says:
the great JG?

alwaysannie says:
JG? really? you should go!

madmaddie says:
psychic chicks! it feels kind of funny though. i
mean, u ppl won't be there will u?

rowdyruth says:
hardly. we're not cool enough for SA!

angelicallyssa says:
so not true. SA just doesn't see quality!

madmaddie says:
thx a lot!

angelicallyssa says:
except for u i mean!

alwaysannie says:
well, do you want to go?

angelicallyssa says:
course she wants to go.

alwaysannie says:
MM, r u in there????

madmaddie says:
sorry. just thinking about ur question. we always
said SA was stuck up and stuff. don't want to be
stuck up too.

alwaysannie says:
give it a chance. maybe we were wrong.

rowdyruth says:
totally

madmaddie says:
seriously? u won't mind?

alwaysannie says:
go, have fun. make JG fall madly, passionately in
love with you. ☺

madmaddie says:
as if

divinedevon says:
hey. ur better than SA any day.

madmaddie says:
thx DD

divinedevon says:
YW. i mean it. JG would be lucky to have u for a
g/f.

madmaddie says:
A g/f!!! just want to say hi to the guy!

rowdyruth says:
u gotta think big!

alwaysannie says:
totally agree with RR

angelicallyssa says:
go to the party. have fun. fall in love.

madmaddie says:
sounds easy! u ppl r the best!

alwaysannie says:
so ur going?

madmaddie says:
k. TYVM u guys. i'm going to do it. i think.

rowdyruth says:
u r!

angelicallyssa says:
BFN

divinedevon says:
GTR...

alwaysannie says:
ttyl

I spent the rest of the week wobbling between excitement and complete terror. Friday night arrived on the scene long before I was ready for it. Have you ever noticed Time has a twisted sense of humor? When you are doing something you need it for, like answering an exam question on the entire history of the world, it flies away from you before you have a chance to breathe. When you are stuck doing something that you desperately want to end, like listening to a teacher tell you about the entire history of the world, Time crawls along, mocking you as you desperately beg it to move forward.

Friday night fell under both categories. I wanted it to come fast, and I didn't want it to come at all. Once it did get there, I didn't know what to do with it.

"Hey, what are you doing?" Annie walked into my room, where I was buried under clothes.

"I am trying on stuff. I don't have anything to wear. I don't have any new clothes so Suzanne has probably seen everything I have and she'll think that I don't have anything else to wear, which I don't!" I kind of whined it, which I am not proud of. I tore off yet another sweater and threw it on the bed. Annie looked a little like she was regretting her offer to come and help me get ready.

"I'm sure you have something nice. I doubt Suzanne has

really paid that much attention to everything you own. I like this one on you," She held out a blue sweater. I put it on, even though I was pretty sure it was a discard from about an hour before.

"Oh, God, this one makes me look like a cow!" Still whining.

"Then someone forgot to feed the animals, because you are a pretty skinny-looking cow!"

"Yeah, well, I've never seen a cow with a butt this big!" I twisted around so that I could see myself in the mirror. I needed one of those three-panel jobs the stores have.

"You obviously haven't seen many cows then, city girl." Annie said, shaking her head a little. She sounded impatient, which I thought was monumentally unfair. I mean, she offered to help.

"I've seen enough cows to know when I look like one! I probably shouldn't go. I wouldn't fit in anyway." I sat down on my clothes pile.

"Maddie, please just put on some clothes and go. You used to make jokes about yourself and it was funny, but now everything is so serious! You really sound like you're going over the edge here."

"Look, I don't need you here if you're going to make things worse. I thought you came to help."

"I am trying. You aren't really making it easy. I don't understand what you're doing."

"I'm sorry. I just want to look perfect." I could feel the tears welling up and tried to fight them back. "I've tried so hard, but I still look fat in everything."

"Maddie, you don't look fat. You can't look fat, because you aren't fat. Just look at yourself!" She took me by the shoulders and stood me in front of the mirror. I looked at myself. Was she blind or just trying to be mean? Couldn't she see how fat I still was? Was she trying to make me feel bad?

"You just don't understand," I said, sniffling.

"You're right, I don't!" Annie looked a little like she wanted to cry too. What did she have to cry about? She had always been skinny, ever since we were kids. She couldn't possibly get it.

"Should I go or not? What if everyone laughs at me?" I asked, even though I was pretty sure she wouldn't have an answer.

"If anyone laughs, you tell them exactly where to go and then you leave. Besides, no one is going laugh. You look great!" She said that because I finally had some clothes actually on. I kept on the blue sweater and matched it with some new, already faded jeans. My mother had a lot of trouble with that concept. She could not figure out why I would want to buy jeans that looked like someone else had already worn them for a year or two. I tried to explain the concept of fashion to her, but my mom still used the word "slacks" when she talked about my pants, so I figured she was a lost cause. I finger-combed my hair and took a deep breath.

"So, am I ready?"

"Yes, you are definitely ready. Have a terrific time...and relax!" Annie gave me a quick hug and headed off for home. I stood for another minute staring at myself in the mirror, willing it to make me smaller. The mirror was uncooperative so I just made myself go downstairs before I chickened out completely.

Steve drove me to Suzanne's huge house in the rich people's subdivision. I could see the glow of lights reflecting off the pool in the backyard. Wow. We had one of those little molded plastic wading pools that we both had outgrown about a zillion years ago. We still filled it up sometimes just to cool our feet off. My whole house would have fit into Suzanne's garage.

"Hey, kid, you're moving up in the world. Be careful and don't do anything that I would do." Steve ruffled my already messy hair, and I slapped his hand away. I gave a quick prayer of thanks to the weather gods that it was too cold for swimming. I was still too gross to go out in public in a bathing suit.

"That whole silent routine is very attractive, kid. Anyway, I'll pick you up at exactly eleven, Mom's orders." I smiled a little and nodded as I got out of the car and stood for a minute watching the car drive away.

I remember I stood on the front porch for what seemed like forever. Time playing his little tricks again. I could hear music that I didn't recognize and lots of yelling and laughing. I looked around the yard a bit, wondering what I was supposed to do. No one would hear me knock but I didn't know anyone well enough to just walk in. I didn't want to stand on the porch for three hours waiting for Steve to come back and rescue me. My problem was solved – or maybe it was just starting – when the door opened and Suzanne came out with her perfect boyfriend, Sean. He was probably the quarterback on the football team or something equally impressive that I can't remember right now.

"Twelve should be enough," Suzanne was saying to him as she kissed him full on the mouth. I tried not to stare. I had only ever kissed my pillow on the mouth and it was always kind of dry and unresponsive. Sean's mouth looked a lot wetter and more enthusiastic.

"Sure, babe, back soon," he said, breaking the clinch and running past without noticing me. I wasn't surprised. Boys never seemed to notice me. He hopped into a tiny red car and roared off with a loud squealing noise. I've often wondered why it seems that only teenage boys are able to make that precise sound when they drive. Do they learn it in Driver's Ed?

"Oh, hi, um, Marty, is it?" Suzanne finally registered that I was there. I nodded like an idiot. Marty's a nice name too. Of course, it wasn't my name, but I wasn't going to quibble.

"Hi," I said, relieved that I could still, apparently, talk.

"Come on in. Sean's just gone home to snag some more beer. His parents stock-pile the stuff. They don't notice when he borrows some, so long as he takes a little at a time. He'll be legal in a month, so we won't have to do this anymore. I can't wait!"

I followed her into the living room, which was completely full of bodies. Every surface seemed to have someone on it, drinking or talking or making out. I saw a few people I recognized from school. Not too many band nerds there. Actually, none that I could see.

Many strangers. I felt instantly and totally out of place and wished with all of my heart that Annie or Ruth or Devon or Alyssa was standing beside me.

"Help yourself," Suzanne was saying, holding an open bottle of beer towards me.

I looked at it in a blind panic. I had never had alcohol in my life. I know that sounds hopelessly nerdy, but it was true. My mom had pounded it into my head that booze was dangerous for young ladies, leading to a loss of control and the possibility of finding oneself in a compromising position with an equally out-of-control boy. She also told me that I would say things I would regret and act like an idiot. Since I already felt like an idiot, I didn't want to start talking like one too. Not that I believed most things my mother said about life anymore, but at the same time, I couldn't be absolutely sure she was wrong about this one. This was not the time or the place to test the theory for the first time. What was I supposed to do? Saying no made me look like a baby and saying yes could make all of my mother's predictions come true, which would give her the ultimate "I told you so" moment and mark the end of my already shaky social life.

"I don't drink beer," I said, a flash of brilliance lighting up my night. "It's too fattening." I held my breath a little, terrified that I had ended my evening right there and then.

"Fattening, eh? Yeah, I read that somewhere. I always thought you just peed it all away, though!" Suzanne laughed and drank about half the bottle in one go.

"No, I think it has, like, two hundred calories or something. Even light beer has over a hundred most of the time," I improvised. I didn't actually know. I'd never looked it up and I didn't have my book on me. I had heard it somewhere, sometime, maybe, perhaps, but I wasn't sure.

"Two hundred, eh? Wow, that's a lot. Maybe I should try something else. How many calories in vodka?" Suzanne seemed actually interested.

"I don't know, but I can look it up," I offered.

"Could you? That would be great. So, you're really into the whole diet thing, aren't you?"

"I guess so." I wasn't sure if that was the right answer or not.

"Do you, like, check the calories in everything you eat?"

"Pretty much," I said, still not sure if I was on the right track. This was the sort of stuff I didn't understand at all.

"Cool. You already lost lots of weight. You still dieting?"

"Sort of." Safe answer.

"Well, good for you. I'll know who to ask for advice if I ever get up the willpower to lose weight!" Suzanne patted her concave stomach. "I'd better go see if Sean's back. Have fun."

I stood there wondering how to do that. I couldn't find anyone to talk to. I wondered where Suzanne's parents might be. They didn't seem to be home. Hmmm.

I guess that would be the point to the Friday night parties. Smart, Maddie – I mean, Marty. My parents would freak if Steve or I ever did anything remotely like have a parentless party.

"Hi."

My thoughts were interrupted by the most gorgeous voice on the planet coming out of an equally gorgeous mouth. I looked up to find Jesse smiling down at me. My heart started pounding like an out-of-control metronome. I was sure he could hear it over all of the party noise and I tried to tell it to be quiet.

"Hi." Snappy comeback, Maddie-Marty.

"Having fun?"

"Oh, yes." Good job. Two whole words.

"Want a drink?" He held out a beer towards me. I didn't think he would be as impressed with the whole calorie-counting excuse as Suzanne so I just kind of nodded like my head had come loose and took it from him. I had forgotten how to talk so I took a long enough drink to try to get my mind under control. Although, in retrospect, sucking back alcohol is likely not the best method of personal mind control.

"Wow, you sure like your beer!" he said, sounding impressed. All this time wondering how to impress guys and all I had to do was down a few gulps of gross-tasting beer. I opened my mouth to see if it still worked and before I could stop it a huge burp flew out. I slapped my hands to my mouth in complete horror. OMG, did I just burp in his face? I just stood there, frozen to the floor as he stared at me for a second. Then he started to laugh and totally shocked me by putting his arm around me.

"Done like a real man!" he said, still laughing. I put my hands down and let out a feminine chuckle or two, praying to whatever gods watch over teenaged girls that I wouldn't burp again. Jesse turned to face me and put both arms around me. I felt flattered and nervous even though I was pretty sure he had had a lot more beer than me and was feeling no pain and likely had no idea who I was.

"You're kind of cute," he said, looking down at me through blurry eyes. Maybe it was my eyes that were blurry. I had downed most of that bottle!

"Thanks. You too," I finally remembered a few words, although apparently my brain was still not part of the equation. You too? Could I be any lamer?

"Thanks," he said, still holding onto me.

Jesse held me pretty close for someone who had never actually looked at me before. He had his hands around my waist so I sort of slid my arms up and put them around his neck. I didn't know what to do next. It was really loud in there and the few words we had managed to spew out were kind of yelled. Was I supposed to try to talk to him over the music? I tried to look around surreptitiously at other couples. Some were laughing and talking, others were making out. Oh, hadn't thought of that. What would I do if he kissed me? Kiss him back? Scream and run?

Where's Annie when I need her? Why wasn't there an instruction book or something? I snuck a peek at Jesse's face. He looked relaxed and unconcerned and didn't seem to be revving up for a kiss. He looked down at me.

"I can't believe how small you are," he said. "I could probably span your waist with just my hands!" He laughed as he tried to do it. His fingers didn't quite make it.

"Not quite that small." He laughed again. The moment ended and Jesse gave me a little salute and went off to do other exciting things. He didn't offer me any more drinks, although a couple of other guys did. I told them no and spent the rest of the night hiding in the shadows and feeling like I wanted to disappear completely, until Time cooperated and my evening finally ended.

I went home at eleven, as promised. I stood in front of the mirror that night and tried to span my waist with my own hands. Not a chance. Jesse was likely grossed out by my flab, which would explain why he had disappeared for the rest of the night. What could I do? Maybe I should start exercising along with the calorie counting. That might work. What kind of exercises should I do? I wasn't what you would call a jock. I knew how to do crunches, sort of. I had my bike, but I could only ride it during the daytime. I didn't always have time for that. I needed something I could do at night. Maybe I should try running or something. We had a treadmill that no one ever used down in the basement. Maybe Devon would take some time and help me get started. Maybe I should take a few minutes and call Devon just to say hi or maybe go online and see if anyone else was up for a chat. They'd all be totally wondering how things went.

I needed to exercise more than I needed to chat, though. I could always catch up with the girls later. I started right then, forcing myself to do about a hundred crunches even though I was really, really tired. If this was going to be my nightly routine, I might as well get used to it. When I finally got to bed, though, sleep was a long time in coming.

As I started to drift off, I wondered what to tell Annie about the party. I was pretty sure she wouldn't understand how I felt about it.

As I fell asleep, I thought about how some words just belong together. Fat and ugly. Thin and beautiful.

No one ever says fat and beautiful.

April 12

I only see my mother on visitors' day once a week and every time she comes she looks all worried but tries to hide behind this big fake smile that makes her look like she belongs in a horror movie. She asks me how I feel and if I am I eating. I smile sweetly and tell her yes, and she looks relieved for a moment. Maybe if I can get her to really believe me, she'll spring me from this place.

But the truth is, I'm not going to start eating all of this crap they're trying to force on me. No one gets it. I can't be fat again. Ever! I couldn't bear it. I can't go back there. Everyone staring at me, judging me. Every time I eat something in public, everyone watching me, thinking to themselves that I shouldn't be eating it, that I deserved to be fat. Thinking I'm weak and stupid.

I can't do it. I can't eat just to please my mother, or Annie, or the Redheaded Menace. I can't do it. It's not safe. I can't let the calories into my body. They'll stay there and turn into fat cells that I can't get rid of. If I get fat again, I'll lose myself and never find myself again. The only way to stop that from happening is to keep the food away. No one understands that. They think I'm being stubborn or hurtful or stupid or something. I'm just doing what I have to do. I'm just keeping myself safe.

There are only three people who get it. Three friends who deserve better than to be dumped by me – even though it wasn't my fault. Three friends who might think I don't want to be part of the group anymore. Friends who might think I've gone back to the shadows. Friends who no one really knows anything about, not even Annie. Especially not Annie.

I don't know, maybe Wolf or Marina would understand. I've seen them both around a bit but neither of them has really tried to talk to me. I mean, Marina did come in that one

time but that's it. I guess I wowed her with my friend-repel-
ling skills. And I guess I haven't tried to talk to them either.
Maybe I should. I just don't know if I can remember how to
be social and friendly and all those things they would most
likely expect me to be.

chapter 9

I felt really weird after the party, like I had stepped into a new version of myself. I didn't know how to explain that to Annie so I didn't even try.

"So?" she said to me that Monday on the way to school.

"So what?" As if I didn't know.

"So, I haven't talked to you since Friday. You weren't online all weekend so I finally called. Didn't Steve tell you?"

"Oh no, I guess he forgot." I sent a silent apology to my brother, who had told me that Annie called. I just didn't want to admit to her that I had deliberately chosen not to call back. I didn't think she would really be all that sympathetic if I told her I was upset because Jesse thought I was fat. She had already made it perfectly clear that she didn't want to talk to me about my body in any sort of helpful way.

"So, come on, tell me about the big party."

"There isn't that much to say. It was noisy and it was crowded."

"That isn't a big surprise. It was a party after all. Did you talk to anyone?"

"Yes, a couple of people."

"Well?"

"Well, what?"

"Maddie, you talked non-stop about that party all last week. Now that you've gone, I can't get two words out of you. What gives?" Annie looked confused. Not that I could blame her. We had always talked about every little thing that happened in our lives, especially when it came to boys.

"Nothing. It was just a dumb party with dumber people all trying to be cool." Including me, but I wasn't going to admit that to her.

"Oh. Did Jesse talk to you?"

"A little."

"And?"

"And nothing. He didn't want to talk to me again and that was it. Listen, I really don't want to talk about it."

I knew I was being really unreasonable but I couldn't seem to stop myself. I had spent all weekend worrying about my huge waistline and surfing the Internet trying to find exercises that would take care of it and then staying up late trying to do all of the exercises at once. I had ignored the girls when they came online to talk to me about it and I felt guilty about ignoring everyone, but I didn't know what to say because I couldn't even explain to myself why I felt so bad. I was tired, confused, and cranky.

"OK. Um. Did you get your math assignment done?" Annie tried to change the subject. She looked a little pissed herself but she was more polite than I was and didn't say anything.

"Some of it. I told you I had a busy weekend!" I snapped. I hadn't told her any such thing. Annie looked at me and closed her mouth and kept it closed for the rest of the walk to school. It was the quietest walk I can ever remember us having.

I got in trouble during math for not having my stupid assignment done and was trying not to scream by the time I walked into the cafeteria for lunch. I didn't actually eat lunch anymore but I liked to sit in there and drink a Diet Coke and catch up on the latest gossip with Annie and the girls. Only that day, I wasn't so sure if Annie and I were actually talking after the way I acted on the way to school. I had avoided talking to the others all weekend and still didn't really want to try to explain how crappy the party ended up being, but at the same time I wanted to be with my friends. I hadn't even asked Devon about the running thing yet. I looked toward their table and Annie gave me a smile so I figured we were OK. Maybe no one would ask about the party. Maybe Annie already told them I was being a nutcase about it. As I headed over, I was stopped by a tug on my sleeve.

"Hi! We figured you'd want to sit with us today." Suzanne Albright had me by the arm and was gesturing towards her table full of cool people, kind of the way I imagine the Queen of England once welcomed knights to her ceremonial feasts.

I'd like to think I hesitated here, torn between my real friends and my brand new I-don't-know-what-to-call-her, but I didn't. I didn't even cast a second glance in their direction.

"Sure!" I said brightly, forgetting that I was in a bad mood.

"So, did you like the party? We saw you talking with Dreamy Jesse!" Suzanne smiled knowingly at the other girls at the table.

"The party was awesome!" I said, with wonderfully feigned enthusiasm. At the time, I didn't think of it as feigned. I thought I was being honest. What a crock. Speaking of being honest, I hoped she hadn't seen me chugging back part of Jesse's beer after my big announcement about not drinking.

"So, what's going on with you and Dreamy Guy?" one of the other girls asked. She reminded me of Keisha from camp, with her shining black hair, designer clothes, and flawless makeup.

"Nothing much. Just talking," I said in what I thought was a casual tone.

"There's no such thing as just talking with a guy like him," Suzanne said to all of her subjects, who nodded at her wisdom as subjects should. "If he spent time with you at the party, he must like you."

"Well, I didn't see him the rest of the night." I tried not to wince at the memory and self-consciously wrapped my arms around my enemy, the waist.

"That doesn't mean anything. Some guys like to take it slow. You know, play hard to get." More wisdom and more nodding. They all looked a little like those bobble-head dolls people stick in their car windows. The thought gave me a wild urge to laugh, which I fought down. The rest of the kingdom seemed to take my silence as agreement and jumped into a major conversation, during which they managed to verbally rip apart pretty much everyone who had been at the party but wasn't at the table into tiny little pieces. Clothes, hair, and relationships, both real and imagined, were all laid out for everyone to review and then tossed to the floor.

I was kind of glad I was at the table. I could only imagine what they'd be saying about me if I was across the room at my usual spot beside Annie. As I thought it, I glanced over to see what she was doing. She seemed to be having a great chat with Ruth and Devon. They were laughing, but probably not at someone else's expense.

"Marty doesn't really drink, do you?" Suzanne was saying. I jumped at the sound of my name, startled that they had apparently moved on to talking about people who were actually sitting there. You really had to stay awake around this bunch! "How many calories did you say were in a beer?"

"Oh, I can't remember exactly. Around two hundred, I think."

"Marty is still on a diet," Suzanne said in a voice that you would normally use when announcing that someone had won an Emmy.

"I guess so." Obviously I had to be still dieting. Couldn't they see me?

"Cool. It must feel good to get so slim."

"Um, yeah, it does, I guess." This time the nods were of approval. They still looked like bobble heads but it felt kind of good to have everyone look at me that way.

"Anyway, Marty, you look great." Suzanne stood up, gathering up her things. How was it that she couldn't remember my actual name but she could remember to say the wrong one every single time? Most of the bobble heads scrambled to their feet, madly packing up their things so they wouldn't be left behind.

"I have to head to the little girls' room to fix my face. Want to come?" She looked at me expectantly. I knew I was expected to go and borrow her lipstick or something, but I had to get my homework done.

"Oh, I know what that's like," Suzanne said when I told her. "See you later."

She and her entourage paraded out of the cafeteria. I looked over to Annie's table but she was gone. I looked at my watch. About half an hour left. Not nearly enough time.

I'd always been a good student. Marks were important to me. Annie always laughed at me and told me to chill out about life, but I couldn't. I had to see those red A's on my papers. But recently, I had been having more and more trouble getting my work done. I kept feeling like I was falling asleep when I was working. I was having more and more trouble concentrating in class. I wondered if I was coming down with something.

The dumbest thing happened that afternoon. I was sitting in English class, listening to Mr. Timmons babble on about verbs or something equally enchanting. I started kind of day-dreaming about more interesting things and all of a sudden I could feel someone shaking me and I could hear everyone laughing. The stupid teacher was calling me Sleeping Beauty and telling me to wake up. It took me almost a full minute to realize that I had actually fallen asleep in class...really asleep, as in REM state and dreams and probably snoring!

I didn't know why I was so tired. I wasn't really going to bed that late but I wasn't sleeping all that well, I guess. My stomach hurt sometimes. I couldn't tell my mother because I didn't want her to send me back to Dr. Doom again. He'd likely tell me I needed brain surgery or something because I was turning stupid along with turning fat. Stupid, fat, and ugly...sounds like a band name.

April 15

I was sitting and trying to write my so-called memoirs, which is what I am expected to do during my "personal goal" time, when I heard a voice from the door of my room.

"Hi." That's what the voice said. It was this really nice voice, all smooth like hot chocolate with whipped cream, but it scared me so much that my laptop slipped off my lap and dropped right onto the floor. I looked at it like an idiot for a minute, as if I couldn't figure out how it got down there. The owner of the voice ran across the room and picked it up. He turned it around a few times, examining it, I guess, to see if I had actually smashed it out of commission or not.

"It looks OK," he said, smiling and handing it back to me. He was probably laughing at me more than smiling and thinking that I was a total dweeb. Which was, of course, accurate. As usual, I lost my ability to speak and I stared at him with what I am sure was a completely brain-dead expression on my face. He kept smiling, or likely silently snickering, and sat down beside me on the bed.

"I'm Pieter," he said, his voice dripping chocolate. I do

love chocolate, even though I only eat it in my dreams where it has no calories.

"Oh, I thought you were Wolf," I said, simultaneously surprised that I had managed to speak and mortified by what I had said. Now he would know I'd been talking about him!

"Most people call me that. Some people call me other things. My real name is Pieter, though."

"I like Wolf," I stammered back, trying to smile sweetly but probably looking like a demented clown. I tried to surreptitiously check my chin for drool.

"Thanks. Me too." He stood looking at me, his eyebrows raised up in a kind of question. He was obviously waiting for me to say something. Oh. Right. My name. What was it again? I couldn't remember it at all in that instant. I thought hard and came up with it a second later.

"Maddie." It kind of flew out of my mouth. I tried to sneak a look at his cheek to check for spit.

"Suits you." Was that a compliment? I wasn't sure but it kind of sounded like one! Now what was I supposed to say? Was I supposed to compliment him too? Should I tell him Wolf suits him? No, that would be stupid. Man, I wish I knew what to say to people – I mean, male people.

"You settling in OK?" he asked, saving me from certain embarrassment.

"Um, yeah, well, sort of, I guess." He didn't seem put off by my total lack of social skills but nodded as if I had actually said something intelligent.

"Yeah, I know what you mean," he said, which startled me

because I didn't think I meant anything at all. "This place can take some getting used to."

"Yes, it can. I don't think I'm used to it at all yet." Wow, a whole sentence. Go, Maddie!

"Maybe they don't want us to get too used to it. They don't want us here long enough to feel comfortable or anything. They would rather have us as outpatients than guests." The last sentence was said in a perfect imitation of the head counselor babe. I laughed. That is what they called us. Guests. Like we wanted to be there because it was so lovely to visit. As if we hadn't been dragged here kicking and screaming by our parents.

"Really? I kind of thought they got us in here and kept us here for life. Have you been a *guest* long?" I put the same twist on the word as he had. He laughed a little too.

"Long enough," was his rather vague answer. Long enough would have been about five minutes for me.

"Oh, are you leaving soon?" I asked, as if it was any of my business.

"I don't know for sure yet. They don't want you here forever but they don't want to let you out before you're ready either. It's not so bad if you have people to hang around with." He stood up. I looked up at him, wondering what to do now. Did he want to hang around with me?

"Well, I guess I'll head off," he said. It was weird actually. He didn't seem a whole lot better at carrying on a conversation than I was. Maybe we needed Marina here to run interference and keep the talking going.

"Actually, I wouldn't mind hanging out some time. This

place can be kind of quiet," I said quickly before I could chicken out.

"Cool." He walked out the door, leaving me clutching my laptop and feeling like I had just climbed a mountain. I had actually, factually, made a real effort to socialize with someone...and I didn't feel totally stupid about it.

I wished I could tell the girls about it. They all would have told me congrats and "go girl" and "you're all that" and all kinds of supportive things. But I don't have them anymore. They're gone just as much as Annie is gone. They're gone just like Devon and Alyssa and Ruth and everyone else I've ever actually thought liked me at all.

I don't really have anyone. Five-minute conversations with strangers don't really cut it.

chapter 10

It was a couple of weeks after the party disaster when I finally realized that my mom literally understood nothing about me. I mean, I had known for a long time that she didn't understand much, but this was the day when I knew she didn't understand anything. It was first thing on a Saturday morning, and I made the mistake of wandering into the kitchen just as she was cooking breakfast.

"Would you like some breakfast?" Mom asked. She was cracking eggs in butter that was bubbling grossly in a pan on the stove. My stomach started to heave at the thought of letting any of those fat cell feeders anywhere near my mouth.

"No thanks, I'm not very hungry this morning," I said. I wasn't lying either. I really didn't feel hungry. I never feel hungry.

"No, you're never hungry, are you?" Mom said, turning down the stove and looking at me. Her eyes looked kind of wet, and she seemed royally ticked off with me. I couldn't for the life of me figure out what her problem was.

"That isn't true," I lied.

"Oh, yes it is. You eat almost nothing and spend every spare minute you have exercising. You're wasting away to nothing, Madison!"

"Oh my God, Mother, stop being so dramatic! I'm hardly wasting away. Look at me!" I could feel my stupid tears coming again and I willed them away. I was good and pissed now. "What is your problem anyway? You sit by all of these years and don't even tell me what a fat pig I'm turning into, then you have a big conspiracy going with Dr. Idiot to have him tell me, and then when I finally manage to lose a few pounds, you get on my case!" I only stopped yelling because I was out of breath. I couldn't believe her!

"A few pounds! Maddie, there is almost nothing left of you. You've lost an enormous amount of weight and you were never a 'fat pig' to begin with. I don't know what you mean about Dr. Fitzroy. I never conspired with him."

"Yes you did! You sent me to that stupid checkup before high school so that he could tell me how disgusting I was!" I wiped a tear that managed to escape and turned away from her.

"No, Madison, that's not it at all. I never thought any such thing! You have always been beautiful and had a lovely figure. Now you're becoming skin and bones."

"Nice, Mom. First I'm wasting away and now I'm skin and bones. Sounds like you're writing a book or something. Some BS teenage help book. Look around you, Mom. The beautiful people in this world are all thin. Turn the TV on, check out the Internet, or read a magazine or two. Welcome to the new millennium. Good bodies are thin bodies. Thin is beautiful. Why don't you want me to be beautiful?"

"Madison, you have always, always been beautiful!" Mom was crying for real now, but I was too revved up to care.

"Yeah, well, that's what you have to say, isn't it? All moms lie to their kids and tell them how gorgeous they are. This is where you do the whole soap commercial thing and tell me that everyone is beautiful in their own way, right?"

"No, but that is what I believe. I do live in the world, Madison. I know that young girls are pressured to be slim. I do watch television and read the occasional magazine. But this isn't television, this is real life."

"Yeah, well, my real life is fat and ugly and I just want to be thin and beautiful."

"You have never been fat or ugly – never!" Mom yelled. That got my attention. No matter how much we fought, Mom almost never actually yelled. She believed in the power of the quiet voice, which, let me tell you, can be pretty scary at times. Right then, though, the loud voice was so unnatural that it shut me up. Mom must have thought I was giving in because her voice got quiet again.

"Honey, I just want you to be healthy and strong. You seem so tired these days. I made you an appointment with Dr. Fitzroy."

"No friggin' way!" I yelled now. "You cannot make me go to him again. I have a newsflash for you. It's my body. Mine! No one can make me eat what I don't want to. Not you, not Annie, not the stupid doctor, not anybody! I decide how I want to look and how I'm going to get there. Understand? It's up to me. Me!" I ran out of the room, ignoring the look on my mom's face. She deserved it. She was being totally unreasonable and unfair and unsupportive and every other "un" word I could think of.

I ran into my room and slammed the door as hard as I could. I went over to my mirror, breathing like I had just been in some kind of race. I looked at myself, panting and red-faced, tears pouring down my cheeks. I lifted up my shirt and looked at my stomach. Mounds of ugly white flab stared back at me.

I grabbed some of it and pinched down hard. That wasn't enough so I worked my way around my waist, pinching and slapping at my fat as if I was trying to scare it away.

After a couple of minutes, I started to feel what I was doing and stopped. I couldn't believe it. Big red welts were forming all over my gut. I started to cry harder. Why had Mom acted that way? This was all her fault!

I must have fallen asleep for a while, because when I looked up it was almost lunchtime. I started down the stairs so that I could sneak out the front door before Mom started the whole food-pushing deal again. I couldn't face another fight. I made it down about two steps when I heard voices, so I stopped to eavesdrop. I knew I should just go back to my room and shut the door, but I could tell that they were talking about me so I decided it was my right to listen.

My dad's voice was all gentle and soft. It's the kind of voice that makes you think everything's OK even when it isn't. He was asking my mother what was wrong. She sounded like she might have been crying but I wasn't sure. I hadn't really heard my mother cry too often so I might have been imagining it.

Mom was telling him about the fight we had over breakfast and saying how she was all worried about me and everything. She started babbling on about me being too thin and thinking I was sick and wanting me to humiliate myself at the doctor's again. I wished she would shut up already and not get my dad all upset too. My dad tried to calm her down and then she started yelling at him about how I have an eating disorder and I need counseling. Dad said something I couldn't hear and then mom started talking about all the danger signs and how obvious it was to anyone who was paying attention. They stopped talking all of a sudden and then I heard my brother's voice telling them he was going over to a friend's house for supper. They both started talking to him about school and other boring stuff so I stopped listening and went to my room.

Eating disorder? So that's what my mom was getting all hot and bothered about. Crazy. All I was doing was trying to lose some weight and have a healthy body and my mother freaks out and drags my dad into it as well.

Obviously my mom didn't really understand what these things were really all about. I knew about eating disorders. We talked about them at school and half the celebrities out there were hanging out at clinics looking like they were starving. As if Mom thought I was like any of them! Even so, I decided to do some research online. The more I knew about it, the quicker I could make my mother understand that she was way off base this time. I could also make sure that her buddy the doctor didn't try to persuade her that there was something desperately wrong with me.

Yes, I decided to go to the stupid appointment. I had a

feeling my poor dad was going to offer to come and ask me to go so that he could stop Mom from freaking out again. He was going to have a tough time doing it and I was going to feel sorry for him and end up giving in anyway. So I just decided to give in right away. It was easier than fighting and besides, I didn't have to listen to anything the so-called medical professional had to say. It was my body. No one could make me change it. Nobody but me.

I've always been a pretty good student, all anal and every-thing when it comes to stuff like research, so I knew I was up to the challenge of getting the straight goods. I started where every good researcher starts...Google. I can't remember when Google turned into a verb. People say stuff like "I'm going to Google that." People amaze me. They all jump on some word bandwagon and decide that something that used to be a brand name has become an everyday word. The only word stupider than "Google" is "Googling." Like "I was Googling the other day and I found something awesome." Googling sounds like something you do just before you choke to death.

Anyway, I typed the words "eating disorder" into the search bar. I got mountains of hits, but the very first one was the ever-faithful Wikipedia. I brought it up and started scrolling through. I read lots of the same old boring information that I remembered vaguely from health class. There's all sorts of confusion about what causes these disorders, which made it seem to me that no one could really agree on what to do about it or how to figure out who needed help and who didn't. There was one section that focused on the physiological nature of eating disorders and what brain chemicals might be out of whack. Another section talked about socioeconomic factors and another about psychological issues. Another part looked at things like perfectionist personalities and body image issues, social pressures and cultural issues. There were all sorts of scary warnings about what could happen to someone with an eating disorder, including actually dying.

It was information overload and seemed to be all over the map in terms of helping anyone figure out whether they had something to worry about or not. I couldn't really see what any of it had to do with me.

It also talked about the Pro Ana sites we had learned about in health class. I remembered the teacher telling us that these were considered a really negative influence on young girls with eating problems. They supposedly said that anorexia and bulimia were a life choice, not a sickness. The message we got was that these sites made sick people sicker. I didn't think much about it at the time. It was just one more piece of information I had to remember for the next health test.

I spent about an hour scrolling around trying to find some information that made sense to me. I was surprised to find that most of the so-called Pro Ana sites had the same kinds of information that Wikipedia had. Lots of medical stuff about the supposed causes and dangers of eating disorders and big disclaimers that the site isn't there to encourage eating disorders. Which actually made sense. Why would anyone encourage an eating disorder? Then again, maybe it was kind of like the warning labels on cigarette packages. I mean, anyone who has a cigarette package in her hands probably already knows that they cause cancer and the ugly pictures on the front of the package aren't going to really be much of a turn off. I was pretty sure that people who went to sites labeled "Pro Ana" probably already had an eating problem.

I noticed some links at the bottom of one of the sites that led to a whole other set of sites. They were called things like Thinspiration and Thinspo. I clicked on a couple. These ones had all sorts of different things and most didn't have any disclaimers or heavy information about disorders. They seemed more designed for ordinary people who wanted to lose weight. Like me.

I opened up about a dozen sites before I found one that really interested me. It was called thinandbeautiful.com. Thin and beautiful. That was exactly what I wanted to be, so I opened it up to see what it was all about. The home page had all kinds of links on it and I didn't know where to start. There seemed to be a bunch of little chat rooms you could go into. It was almost like there were different clubs you could join, each with its own name. I looked them over and was kind of intrigued by one called girlswithoutshadows, so I opened it up. It had this little blurb on the home page that said:

"We have been in the shadows of our oversized bodies for too long and it is time to come out into the sunlight. It is time to find our true, thinner self and to dispel the shadows of self-doubt, self-loathing, and self-consciousness. It is time to create a body that will no longer cast a shadow on the ground."

It sounded pretty dramatic, but at the same time kind of true. I did feel like no one could really see me anymore, like I was still sitting in the shadowy corners at Suzanne's house watching everyone else have fun. The site had one of those forums where you can read other people's posts without participating so that you can decide if you want to be in it or not. I decided to take a look and see what people outside of my little narrow-minded world were thinking.

It's kind of weird reading other people's conversations, like peeking through a window at someone's private life. I guess the difference is that these people have left their windows open on purpose so that people can look in.

bodaciousbod says:
my boyfriend is taking me out tonight for supper.
i haven't eaten all day so i can save up some
calories for alcohol. man, i can't wait!

nevertoothin says:
i am staying in tonite. i feel disgustingly fat
today. mom baked chocolate chip cookies and looked
like she was going to cry so i ate one. tried to
get rid of it but it wouldn't go so now it's stuck
in there. i feel like cutting it out with a knife.

bodaciousbod says:
did anyone find out the actual calorie count of
movie theater popcorn? my date starts in an hour
and i know he's going to buy some and try to get
me to eat it!! i haven't eaten since yesterday but
i'm still not sure if it's safe to eat.

lookingforlight says:
just take one piece at a time and chew real slow,
and spit it out when he isn't looking. hey, did
everyone see SR? i posted some pics so that we can

all see real beauty. i can't believe everyone's
freaking and thinking she needs help. i wish i
had her kind of help. i heard she weighs like 87
pounds. she's awesome.

nevertoothin says:
i am so much bigger than that! i have to stop
eating…now! i am so disgusting today I'll have to
change my name to alwaystoofat. no one understands
it at all…well, except all of you guys!

I clicked on the link they were talking about. The pictures came up. I had seen some of them before in the magazine rack at the grocery store. She was definitely thin and beautiful. Her cheekbones stood out sharply and her blue eyes looked absolutely huge. Her hair was perfect and straight and blond...the opposite of mine. She didn't look unhappy with herself at all. I wondered about the eighty-seven pounds part. Could she be that little? I didn't think that eighty-seven pounds looked like that. I weighed a lot more than that. Maybe that's why I felt so fat. Maybe those pictures would inspire me after all.

I couldn't add any comments to the gallery because I wasn't a member. I read them all though. Some of the comments seemed a little weird and over the top. Some of the girls really had a hate-on for themselves! I guess they still had some of their shadows. They seemed to speak to me though. I had had lots of the same kind of thoughts and it felt good to know that other people felt the same way. I mean, even though Suzanne and people like her seemed to think I was kind of cool for doing my diet stuff, they still didn't really understand me.

I couldn't actually talk to any of them about it.

Then again, I wasn't sure if I was ready to talk to any of the online girls either.

Did I really want to be a member of a chat group? It seemed like such a good way to get to know other girls who felt like me. Maybe they could tell me what to do with my mom to get her off my case. Who knows, maybe I would even learn something.

But what if I didn't fit in?

April 18
I had a dream last night. I dreamed about chocolate. I know. It's lame. I have always dreamed about food. It's almost like my subconscious mind wants to eat more than my conscious one does. This actually works out in my favor because dream food is nonfattening. Anyway, my chocolate dream was smooth and tasty and full of flavor. I was savoring it melting in my mouth when all of a sudden the chocolate turned into Wolf. No, that's not right. It wasn't like there was a chocolate guy melting in my mouth. It's just that the tastes and flavors turned into a real life-sized chocolate version of Wolf. That sounds just as stupid. That's one dream I would never tell anyone about. Especially not Marina, who came walking into my room about five minutes after I woke up.

"So?"

"So what?" I asked, yawning widely and not bothering to cover my mouth. My mom wasn't around so I didn't need manners.

"I know he came here to talk to you yesterday. D'you like

him?" She plopped herself down on the bed like she was right at home. She sat cross-legged in the middle of my blankets, making me shift over. I rubbed my eyes, trying to wake up and trying not to think about embarrassing chocolate dreams in front of someone who would most likely laugh hysterically if she found out about them.

"I don't know. He didn't say much."

"No, he's not really a stimulating conversationalist. Then again, do you know any guys his age who are?" She shook her head and kind of rolled her eyes. I noticed her hair stayed perfect when she moved, like a sleek cap of black silk or something. I knew my hair was a bird's nest in the morning and I resisted the temptation to smooth it down. I thought about her question for a moment.

"Actually, no, I don't," I said, kind of surprised at my own answer. I always thought that I was the conversation dweeb. But when I really thought about it, most of the boys I knew didn't really have all that much to say either.

"No, I don't think there are any. I think they have to get a whole lot older before they have anything to say. I definitely like older guys. What about you?"

"Don't know. I don't think I know any older guys except my brother, and he doesn't count."

"Hmm, is he cute?"

"Gross – that's my brother you're talking about! No, he's not cute!"

"Not to you, maybe. Does he come here on visiting day? I could use some new distractions."

"Cut it out. You'll make me puke, which will get me in

trouble because they'll think I did it on purpose."

"Yeah? Have you got caught?" she asked with interest. She didn't look like she thought it was gross, which I guess shouldn't surprise me. I couldn't be the only purger in here or they wouldn't have so many rules and consequences for it.

"Yeah. Shocked the hell out of me too. I'm so good at it. My parents didn't catch me for months."

"They have mysterious ways around here that I haven't figured out yet. But I will. I treat this place like a big reality game show. A me-against-them kind of thing. Keeps me amused."

I looked at her, feeling something close to shock. It was like my attitude about this place was looking in a mirror at itself.

"The only game worth playing is the one where you get to make all the rules and not tell the other players," I said, half grinning at her for the first time. She grinned back.

"Totally. Maybe this can be an *us*-against-them kind of thing now. We might have more of a chance then. Anyway, I'm heading, so you can get up. They won't be too happy if you stay in bed all day. You'll have to go to the excessive lack of energy therapist and discuss your lack of energy until you're so tired you fall asleep." She unfolded herself and stood up in one movement that kind of flowed off the bed. I still had half a grin on my face as I watched her walk out of the room and go off to wherever it was that she spent her time.

Someone who thought a little bit like me. Here of all places. Us against them instead of just me.

chapter 11

The clouds came out in full force the day of my appointment, which seemed appropriate for my mood. Isn't that called pathetic fallacy or something? Anyway, it was definitely pathetic. My parents were so pleased that I agreed to go that I even briefly felt guilty that I had already made my mind up not to listen to anything the jerk said. The guilty feeling left me about thirty seconds into the poking and prodding and weighing, however.

Once he had finished and I was dressed again, I waited for him to come back with his little chart and tell me that I still had to watch the food I put in my mouth. I sat with arms folded and legs crossed, making sure he knew I wasn't about to be impressed by anything he had to say.

"Madison," he started as he walked in the room without even looking at me. "Your weight is down to ninety-three pounds. That's a twenty-seven-pound weight loss since I last saw you."

"So?" I wasn't giving him anything. Twenty-seven pounds?

Was that all? My mother hated scales so I had only been able to weigh myself if I got a chance at other people's houses where they weren't as uptight as Mom. Every scale I tried had me at a different weight and, until this moment, I actually didn't have a very good idea of how much I weighed.

"So, you are becoming quite underweight for someone your age and height. It's a cause for concern."

I was annoyed out of my planned silence. "I don't see why!" The nerve of the guy! "You're the one who said I was fat in the first place! Now you say I'm too thin. Make up your mind!" My mother would have passed out if she heard the way I was talking to him.

"I said what?" The doctor pretended to be confused.

"Last year when I came here you told me to watch what I put in my mouth. So I did. Now you get on my case like everyone else does. You're all nuts."

"Madison, I certainly never told you that you were overweight. I tell many young ladies that they may want to start watching what they eat once their bodies stop growing upwards. As the body slows its growth patterns, sometimes young people find themselves less able to eat every little thing they want without gaining unwanted pounds. The suggestion to watch what you eat was intended to encourage healthy eating, not strict dieting. There is nothing in here about you having any issues with your weight." He was checking my chart, as if looking for some magic words that would solve the puzzle.

"Well, it sounded like that to me. I already knew I was fat, anyway. You just confirmed it. I found out everyone was thinking I needed to lose weight, and they were all so frigging happy when I started to. Now the same people have decided I'm underweight. Make up your mind!" I knew I was repeating myself but I was too mad to think of new things to say.

"I have made up my mind. I am concerned about you. Do you eat at every meal?"

"Mostly." I returned to my vow of almost silence.

"What do you usually eat for breakfast?"

"Juice, food."

"And for lunch?"

"Lunch stuff."

"Do you sleep through the night?"

"Usually."

"Do you vomit?"

"What?"

"Vomit, purge, throw up what you've eaten."

"I know what vomit means. It's just a dumb question. I don't have the flu."

Actually, I knew exactly what he meant. He was trying to figure out if I was doing the whole bulimia thing. But I wasn't. I hadn't tried it. It sounded gross to me.

"When did you have your last period?" He just kept firing the questions at me and recording my non-answers on his little chart.

"I don't know. I don't keep track. I'm not pregnant if that's your worry."

"Madison, I have someone I'd like you to talk with. She specializes in working with young girls who are having some difficulties with eating and body image."

"I am not having a problem with eating and I can see my

body just fine. What I do have is a doctor problem and a parent problem. The problem is that they won't all stay out of my personal business!" I got up and basically stomped out of the room. I tried to slam the door but it wasn't the slamming type, so I just stomped harder on my way out to the car. I realize that wasn't the most mature behavior I could have come up with, but I was seriously ticked off and couldn't come up with anything more creative. I went out to the car where my mother was waiting. She had wanted to come in, but I had told her no. It was bad enough she had guilted me into this at all.

"So?" she asked.

"So what?" Why do people keep setting me up for my favorite non-answer?

"So, what did the doctor say?"

"Nothing."

"Madison, he must have said something." Mom was trying to keep her voice calm and patient but I could hear the edge of something else in there.

"He said that you should back off and leave me alone!" I said impatiently and not very calmly. I closed my eyes and leaned against the window, keeping my body as far away from my mother as I could. I knew that she didn't believe me and was disappointed in me. I didn't like to disappoint her but I wasn't going to see any counselor lady or anyone else who was going to try to tell me how to live my life.

When we got home, I ran up to my room without saying anything more to Mom.

I slammed my door, which was momentarily satisfying, and turned on my computer. I had saved the thinandbeautiful.com site to my favorites. My computer was password protected so I knew no one else could go on and find out what I was doing. Not that I was doing anything wrong. I had the right to chat with other girls about issues that interested me. I wasn't looking at porn or anything. But I still knew that my parents, and even Annie, wouldn't understand.

This time I decided to create a username and password, which would make me a free member and let me actually sign in to the site. All of the other girls had creative handles, so I had to come up with something equally brilliant so that I would fit in. My first choice would have been thinandbeautiful, because that's what I really wanted to be. Except that it was already the name of the website and I would look like a total uninspired idiot if I used it. What I needed was some of what Devon always called "divine inspiration." I'm pretty sure that's where her online name came from. divinedevon. divinemaddie. No way. I wasn't using my real name on this site. No one did. It was like we were all finding a way to be someone else for a while.

I thought for another minute or three and then laughed as the thought hit. I typed it in and wasn't surprised to see it go through, because I was pretty sure no one else would have come up with this one. Of course, that didn't necessarily mean that it was a good one. It could mean that it was so lame that no one else wanted it! I really hoped the other girls wouldn't think it was totally pathetic. I was also hoping it would make them think I really wanted to be part of the group.

divinethinspiration...the new me.

April 23

"Hi!" I said, startled out of my mind by the sight of Wolf sitting in my room when I came back from a counseling session. I just love those sessions. I sit there staring at the so-called counselor and she sits there smiling at me with the world's dumbest smile, trying to get me to talk to her and say something that would make her feel like she's curing me. Since I don't have a real disease, I can't exactly be cured, now can I?

So I just sit there and stare at her until her smile starts to kind of disappear into her wrinkles and she gets frustrated with me. She doesn't say she's frustrated with me, which I'm sure she learned not to do in Counseling 101. She just looks all gentle and kind and tells me that we can try again tomorrow. Like she's offering me a favor or something, as if I actually want to sit there with her tomorrow. At least it wasn't Big Red.

Actually, maybe she doesn't have the world's dumbest smile. I probably have the corner on that one. At least that's probably what I had plastered on my face when I walked in and found Wolf in my room. I could feel the corners of my mouth stretching. It's kind of a strange feeling, because I don't smile much these days. It felt kind of alien, like someone was molding my face for me. I wanted to reach up and feel my cheeks to see if they had turned into Play-Doh. I managed to stop myself from doing it, which was a good thing because I already looked stupid enough standing there with a stupid grin smeared across my face.

"Been to counseling?" Wolf asked. He was smiling also, but he didn't look like his face was going to stretch completely out of shape.

"Yeah. Well, not counseling. It was just a little chat. You know. The whole, come-on-in-with-me-and-we'll-chat-awhile routine, which really means I want to shrink your brain and make you enlarge your body." I stopped talking, a little startled by all those words. I cringed inside a bit. Maybe he liked "chats" and would be offended. Maybe he would think I was a whiner or a complainer or just dumb or something. Maybe he'd walk away and never come back because I opened my big mouth. Maybe he was talking and I was too busy "maybe-ing" to listen to what he was saying!

"I know what you mean. I used to feel that way when I first got here."

"I mean, who is she anyway? She should have to show us her therapist badge like the cops do so we know she's qualified or something."

Wolf laughed at my feeble joke, which made my Play-Doh face stretch out again into a smile. I even opened my mouth and laughed a little.

"That's a good idea. We could try putting it out there at the next group. Oh, right, I've never actually seen you at a group session, have I?"

He was right. I don't go to group sessions. I have enough trouble trying to figure out why I have to go to the stupid one-to-one chat sessions. Why would I want to talk to a whole bunch of losers about the fact that there isn't anything wrong with me that a good escape plan wouldn't fix. Although, I was beginning to think that I would actually have to do the group thing eventually because they weren't going to let me out if I didn't. I hated that cooperation could be my only salvation.

"No, I don't do group sessions just yet," I answered, trying to sound sure of myself and ending up sounding kind of whiny.

"Well, I actually kind of like the group time. When I first came here, I felt really alone, you know? It was tough for me because, as you may have noticed, I'm a guy and there aren't too many of us in this place."

"Yeah, Wolfman, I think she noticed." Marina walked in and plopped herself down. "You don't have any boobs. Not that most of the girls in here have them anymore either." Wolf looked less than totally thrilled to see her and just stood there looking at her. I should have minded her barging in but I didn't. I was actually kind of glad to see her.

"Yeah, the whole eating disorder thing seems to be a girl thing. I mean, if you believe that there is such a thing as an eating disorder at all," I said, to break up the silence.

"You don't think you have an eating disorder? Why else would you be here?" Wolf asked.

"I'm here because other people *think* I have an eating disorder."

"Good answer. I like that. I'm going to use it," Marina said, getting another glare from Wolf.

"Well, I know I have one. No one figured it out because I am a guy, and even though guys can have them, no one thought I did. At least, not at first."

"So you think you have a disorder like they keep trying to tell us we have?" I tried to keep the disbelief out of my voice. I mean, I guess I kind of knew that most of the people stuck in this place had to have something seriously wrong, but Wolf and Marina seemed pretty normal, like me. But then again, I was no judge. I wasn't even the jury. I couldn't decide other people were OK just because I was.

"I do now. I resisted it at first, big time. I told anyone who'd listen that they were all full of crap. Man, I was rude!"

"You, rude? Why, Wolfman, you disappoint me," Marina said, her voice sickeningly sweet.

"You'll see just how rude I can be if you don't shut up," he said rudely. They talked to each other like Steve and me on a bad day.

"Careful, Maddie will think badly of us."

"Sorry, Maddie. Anyway, I just think people need time to figure it out."

"I don't need time. I know I don't have one of those disorder things. I'm fine just the way I am. My parents are the ones who think I'm sick. Maybe they have the disorder. I'm fine." I said that twice, didn't I? I was getting all worked up and I could feel my face turning a lovely shade of crayon red.

"You go, girl," Marina said softly. I looked at her and was annoyed to find my eyes tearing up. It was like one of my girls had stepped out of cyberspace for a second and talked to me. At the same time, I realized that I was probably being rude to Wolf and was ruining the start of whatever it was that was starting. I tried to backpedal.

"I don't want you to think that I'm telling you that I don't think you can get helped here just because I can't. I mean, everyone is different, right?" Oh man, just stop talking, Madison! Close your mouth and just get off the bike!

"Right. I'm sorry if I was being pushy or something," he said.

Marina patted him on the arm like a pet poodle. "S'OK, Wolfie, she'll forgive you. I'll forgive you, too."

"It is OK. You can say what you want. I just...I don't like talking to strangers about my life. Especially when my life is just fine." I should really just sew my mouth shut.

"Hey, no worries. You do what works for you. I have to go and talk to strangers now. See ya." He walked out. I watched him leave and just kind of sighed.

"That went well," Marina said with a grin.

"Oh, shut up!" I said and then started to really laugh for the first time since I walked through the "guesthouse" doors.

chapter 12

It really hit the fan with Annie about two weeks after the whole botched doctor's appointment. I still have trouble believing it happened. I don't know if I can even remember it right because it still gets me so steamed.

In the weeks after the appointment, I managed to navigate my way around the website and was starting to think about actually adding my two cents to the chat room. I wasn't sure that I had anything remotely helpful and interesting to say though, so I was still mostly just reading what other people thought. Every once in a while, a message beep would interrupt my reading, letting me know that Ruth, Annie, Alyssa, or Devon were trying to talk to me. I knew I should have taken the time to talk to them, but I was busy and didn't want to lose track of what I was doing. Most of the time I ignored the beeps, telling myself I would talk to them later. Eventually, I just turned the messenger service off so I wouldn't feel guilty.

There was talk about purging by a couple of the girls on the site. I knew that lots of people did it, but it all seemed kind of gross still to me. I mean, I hated puking when I was actually sick and I had trouble imagining doing it on purpose. I couldn't even figure out how it would actually work. I mean, putting your finger right down your throat? Wouldn't that just choke you?

I shuddered at the thought of it. One girl also talked about ways that you could control your stomach muscles so that you could actually make yourself heave and throw up. It said you would still kind of gag the way you do when you have the flu but you would get rid of the calories so it was all worth it. I kind of doubted it. I thought I'd rather not eat the garbage in the first place than have to get rid of it later in the toilet.

I didn't know at the time that I'd become the vomit master.

The other method they talked about is not even worth mentioning but I'll say it anyway. Laxatives. Yeah, that's what I said. Those things that make the food come out the other end, complete with cramps and mad dashes to the toilet. Not my idea of a good time.

Reading the chat room entries later, I was amazed at the girls who used both methods almost every day. They talked like it was normal. It wasn't like they had bulimia or some sort of out-of-control disease. They were just choosing to purge as a way to control their calories.

lookingforlight says:
i ate so much over xmas that I had to pop the choc tabs majorly. i was in the bathroom for like an hour but it cleaned me out so all's good.

nevertoothin says:
i pigged out at my grandma's house and couldn't
get it out of my fat gut so I had to go that way
too. i had major cramps this time but i deserved
it. i shouldn't have had gravy on my potatoes.
actually, i shouldn't have had the potatoes! what
was i thinking? i guess i just couldn't disappoint
my grandmother. good thing I stocked up before we
went. lol

bodaciousbod says:
my throat hurts a little today from the two finger
tango. i had such an xmas binge that I had to go
at it about five times. i think i'm back to normal
though.

nevertoothin says:
cool. nothing like the holidays to make u work!! i
don't think i gained anything but didn't lose it
either.

lookingforlight says:
don't worry about it. u can just be extra careful
now.

nevertoothin says:
hard not to worry when i look like a pig.

I was so engrossed in reading that I didn't hear the door
open behind me and completely missed the quiet footsteps
walking across the room.

"What are you reading?" Annie's voice made me jump out

of my skin. I was too startled to lie so I told her the truth. She looked at me as if I had just told her that I had decided to fly to Mars on the next shuttle.

"This is a website for people who think it's OK to throw up when they're not sick?" she asked, clearly confused and not too impressed. Annie and I weren't ever going to agree about the whole weight thing. It almost felt like we were strangers when we tried to talk about it. I had never thought that there would be anything that we couldn't talk about or at least agree to disagree on. But it seemed to me that our only chance to stay friends was to keep this topic off the table. We just couldn't talk about it without emotions getting in the way, hers and mine. So the last thing on earth I wanted to speak to her about was my new cyber group. I didn't have a clear enough idea of what I thought yet to defend it to her.

"The website is not just about puking, Annie. Don't judge things you don't understand. This is a just a site for people who want to lose weight. There's nothing wrong with that!" I sounded like a petulant baby, even to my own ears, but I couldn't seem find another voice.

"Maddie, this is one of those 'Pro Ana' sites that we learned about in health class. Don't you remember? They encourage people to keep losing weight until they look like skeletons. They show pictures of super thin people and say they're fat and try to tell you that you need to get thinner and thinner. Don't you remember?" She was shaking her head and kind of grabbing herself around the arms as if she was trying to give herself a hug.

"You don't know what you're talking about, Annie. I've

read the Pro Ana stuff and this is definitely not one of those sites. Pro Ana sites are for people who already have anorexia. Which I don't. This is just a site for people who want to lose weight but are having trouble and need help. It's a place where people with the same lifestyle can talk to each other. It's just helping me understand myself a little better and making me feel less alone."

"It's just another way of saying the same thing, Maddie. Can't you see that?" She looked at me. Obviously she could tell from my face that I didn't agree with her so she tried another tactic. I tried the silent treatment to get her to stop. I didn't want to go down this road with her. She didn't take the hint.

"You said the site makes you feel less alone. Why do you feel alone? I'm here for you, Maddie. We've been friends forever. Ruth and Devon and Alyssa want to see you too. They say you barely talk to them anymore. You're never online and you basically just say hi in the hall at school." Her voice had changed into the one she used to use when we were little and she was trying to talk me into something like collecting worms. I wasn't buying it.

"No they don't. They don't try to see me. They don't understand me. And you aren't really here for me. You argue with me any time we talk about this. You haven't been supportive at all. No one has."

"I am being supportive. We don't argue all the time. I'm your friend and I don't want you thinking you're fat when you're not. I don't want you to be sick. This stuff" – she gestured at the computer screen – "is going to make you worse."

"Make me worse! Worse than what? What is wrong with me? I'm so bad that you don't want me to get worse?"

"Madison, you need someone to talk to about this. Talk to your mom."

"My mom understands less than you do. Maybe you can talk to your mom about stuff, but not everyone can. Besides, I don't need to talk to anyone about it. There is no 'it' to talk about."

"I don't know what to say to you." Annie stood for a moment, looking kind of lost.

"Then leave," I said, rudely gesturing towards the door.

I figured that was the end of it and that we had finally kind of agreed to disagree. I thought Annie would come to her senses a little and eventually try to listen to me, or at least stop trying to tell me what to do. Two days later at school, I found out how wrong I was.

Mrs. Taylor, the gym-slash-health-slash-guidance teacher, called me into her office. She sat me down with this big fake understanding look on her face and told me that she was worried about me.

"Why would you worry about me? I'm not even in your class this term," I asked, confused.

"Well, Madison, I've seen you in the halls and I've noticed that you have become very thin. People are worried and I was just wondering if you wanted me to help you find someone to talk to."

Someone to talk to? Where did she get the idea that I needed someone to talk to? Wait a minute. I knew what was happening here. I couldn't believe it, but it was the only explanation. I had heard those same words very recently from a soon-to-be former friend.

"Thanks, Mrs. Taylor, but I'm fine. My mom is helping me and I have a doctor who is working with me also." I lied smoothly, knowing that would be the best way to shut her up. I was right, and she smiled cheerfully, wishing me well as she ushered me out of her office. I bet she was relieved that she didn't have to spend more than thirty seconds with me and could move on to invading someone else's privacy. I stormed down the hall and into the cafeteria, where I found Annie sitting at our table with the other girls. I ignored the fact that they all seemed kind of happy to see me. They'd probably all been talking about me, good old Annie filling them in on my private business and sharing her opinion that I had some big problem. After all, if she'd tell a teacher she wouldn't hesitate to tell the girls. I wasn't happy to see anyone. I wasn't interested in anyone else's opinion. I was pretty sure I wouldn't find any understanding at this table. I stood in front of Annie and glared at her.

"I need to talk to you. Outside. Now!"

Annie looked at me for just a second and got up and followed me outside. Ruth got up as if to follow, but I saw Devon shake her head. Fine. I didn't want anyone else there anyway. I was pretty sure no one was going to be on my side.

"I can't believe you, Annie! How could you do that? And don't pretend you don't know what I'm talking about. You are the only person who could have said anything to Taylor that would get her all up in my face like that!" I was hissing at her in a furious whisper that I was hoping wouldn't attract any attention from the few people wandering around the front steps of the school.

"I'm sorry I upset you. I didn't know what else to do. I'm so worried about you."

"Worried? Maybe you're just worried that I'm going to look better than you or something. Maybe you just like it better when I'm fat!"

"That's ridiculous. Of course I don't want anything like that!"

"No? Well, I think you do. Maybe you liked having a fat friend because you could feel superior or something. Maybe you're not so interested in me anymore because I don't look so different from you now."

"Maddie, that doesn't even make sense! You've always looked different from me. You've always been prettier than me."

"Right. It's a little late for compliments!"

"I don't compliment you. I haven't for ages. If I do, it makes you angry."

"Whatever. All I know is you have been totally unsupportive from the beginning. You dissed me again the other day and you're doing it now. You're worse than my parents and they're bad. Why can't you all accept that I need this? Everyone wants to be thin and beautiful! Why should I be any different?"

"You always say those words together like that as if they're one big word – thinandbeautiful. I don't see anything beautiful about bones showing and getting sick."

"Oh, now I'm ugly and sick. Thanks."

"I didn't say that! You keep twisting everything inside out!" Annie threw her hands up in frustration.

"You know what? Let's just not talk to each other for a while, OK? I don't want your opinion and I don't want you interfering in my life. Got it?" I glared at her, trying not to cry. I wouldn't look as fierce if I cried and I wanted to look fierce so that she would know I meant what I said.

"Got it."

Annie didn't try not to cry. Tears were rolling down her cheeks, and time stood still for a moment while she looked at me before slowly walking away. I stood there, breathing heavy like I had just jogged around the school. I could feel the tears force their way out from under my eyelids and I turned and ran before anyone could see.

April 25

"Sometimes, when I'm at a restaurant, I'm afraid to order things off the menu because I'm sure the waitress thinks I'm too fat to eat it and will go back into the kitchen and laugh about me."

"I know that feeling. I used to feel that way in the cafeteria too. I never wanted to put anything on my tray because I thought everyone was looking at me and judging me for what I was eating and talking about me at their tables."

"But people do judge you! Everyone talks behind everyone else's back all of the time and not to say nice stuff. Everyone talks about people's hair and clothes and how fat or thin they are. It never stops!"

"Totally. I don't know why people have to do that."

"But you know what? Sometimes I do it too, and I don't even think about it. I mean, as long as I'm not the one they're talking about, it's all good, I guess. Does that make me a bad person?"

"No, I don't think so. It probably makes you normal."

"Normal? I don't think anyone is normal. Especially around here!"

Everyone around the circle laughed. Yes, I said circle. I had decided to go to the group thing just out of curiosity. At least that's what I told myself. It had nothing to do with feeling guilty about the way I had talked to a certain someone. I had to formally declare myself ready to be involved in the group schedule and get permission first.

Being in the group schedule meant attending the circle time but also the after-supper debriefing session held every night. Gag me. Oh well, I was getting tired of the whole individualized thing. It actually invited too much attention from the people I wanted to avoid anyway.

So I got my permission, along with lots of congratulations on my great progress, gag me again, and I went to the "sunroom," as they called it, at 10:25 and stood outside feeling stupid. I kind of shrank myself back into a corner to watch the others go in. There were only about four or five of them, all girls at first.

They all looked pretty normal to me, although a couple of them were a little scrawny. They all seemed like they knew each other and didn't look at all freaked out about going to group. I couldn't figure out what I was doing there at all. I didn't know anyone but Wolf, and he didn't seem to be there.

Marina obviously didn't do the group thing, either, because she was nowhere to be seen. I was about to slink my way back to my room when my dream voice spoke just behind me.

"I'm glad you came," he said, melted chocolate dripping into my ears.

"Well, I can't say the same for me," I whispered. I don't know why I whispered exactly. Maybe I was hiding.

"Come on in with me. We can sit in the back on one of their comfy couches and just listen for today. It'll be OK." Wolf held out his hand for me to take. I was sure mine was sweating like the proverbial pig and I wished I could wipe it off on something before touching him. I decided that that would look beyond lame so I just decided to make the best of it and grab hold. I let him lead me into the room. I had never been there before. I could see why they called it the sunroom. It was actually kind of nice, all filled with windows that let in the sunlight. It was painted a creamy yellow that made me think of lemonade in summer. Diet lemonade in summer, I should say. Anyway, there were lots of cushy-looking couches against the walls and a bunch of armchairs arranged in a circle in the middle of the room. There was no TV or anything but there was a piano at the far end of the room. That was kind of interesting. Maybe I could find a time when no one was around to play a tune or two. Or maybe not – I wasn't here to enjoy myself, after all. Not that I actually enjoyed playing the piano anymore. I used to love it back before everyone decided I was going to be a concert pianist someday and started pressuring me to be better and better. I wanted to do what everyone thought I could. I wanted to be the best at it. I really tried. But

I always froze up when I had to play in public. It was like my brain and fingers had a fight and wouldn't work together with other people watching. I couldn't win any of the competitions. I just kept trying and failing. At least that's the way I saw it at the time. I kept on practicing and practicing, hoping that one day I would get my act together and make everyone's dream come true. I used to really love hearing the music coming out of my fingers. After a while, all I could hear were the mistakes.

The five girls were already in there and were chatting with each other, looking pretty comfortable in those chairs. The counselor was there also. Unbelievably, it was the Redheaded Menace. Was she the only one who worked around this place? She was sitting in the same kind of chair as the girls and was just kind of watching everything. I had imagined that she would be carrying a clipboard or something, on which she'd make copious notes while the girls were baring their souls, but she was empty-handed. Probably empty-headed as well. Not that I'm judgmental or anything.

She looked around the circle. I felt myself kind of shrink back into the couch, figuring she'd pick on me because I was the new kid. But she didn't look at me at all. One of the other girls started talking about restaurants and the conversation took off from there. I was surprised to hear them talk about things that I had felt myself and even more surprised that they could laugh at themselves. I kept looking at the counselor babe, expecting her to interrupt with words of wisdom, but she just kind of sat there with a little smile on her face, nodding once in a while. It was as if the girls were in charge of the group and were really just getting together for a chat...kind of like my cyber pals but without the computer screen. No one paid much attention to me and I found myself sinking into their conversation a little.

"Well, we may not be normal, but at least we aren't alone. I used to think I was losing my mind. I mean, my whole family was telling me I was acting nuts, and my friends didn't understand me."

"I know what you mean. My mom tried yelling at me, reasoning with me, pleading with me and being all calm and understanding. Except that she didn't understand. I mean, I wasn't trying to upset anyone. I just couldn't eat, you know? I couldn't do it."

"Me either. I still can't even though I'm here. I want to please everyone but I just can't do it. I don't want to be fat again."

"I felt that way at first too. The first time I weighed myself and found out I had gained a pound I wanted to die. Really. I was afraid to eat for two days! But it's getting a little better. I've gained a little and I'm kind of OK with it. Maybe."

The other girls looked at the one speaking and nodded a bit. I couldn't tell if they were approving of her or just glad that they weren't the one gaining weight. The things they were saying were somehow familiar to me, and for just a second I thought it might be nice to be part of the conversation. I looked at Wolf to see what he thought about it, only to find out that he was gone. I hadn't even noticed him leave. Great, the mighty man-killer strikes again. I couldn't even hold on to a guy in a place full of locked-in, disordered girls. Pathetic.

chapter 13

I didn't always feel like a girl back in grade ten, especially when my period stopped. Maybe I should say that I felt like a little girl again. It was pretty weird. I knew I wasn't pregnant because I was a total and complete virgin. A total and complete virgin is different from your basic virgin in that such a creature has never done anything remotely sexy with a boy. Unless I was going to be on the cover of the *National Enquirer* as the newest Mary, I was pretty sure I couldn't be pregnant from a hug or sharing a beer. I knew that there were some diseases that stopped your period. I also had read somewhere that dieting could do that. After a couple months, I decided it was time to ask the experts.

I logged on to the site and took a deep breath. It was silly but I felt almost as nervous as I had at Suzanne's party. I wanted these girls to like me. Even though they would never actually see me. Maybe that was the good part.

divinethinspiration says:
hi

lookingforlight says:
hey a newbie. nice handle.

divinethinspiration says:
u don't think the name is lame?

bodaciousbod says:
ha ur a poet. no, ur name has to be u. if u like it
that's cool. we'll just call u dt. everyone's on?

lookingforlight says:
yes. hey, dt, we meet here every day at 11. we try
anyway.

bodaciousbod says:
yeah. always good to have newbies.

divinethinspiration says:
thx. i've been reading. hope thats OK.

lookingforlight says:
totally. nothing to hide. nowhere to hide. lol

bodaciousbod says:
all friends here. no secrets. no judgments. no
shadows.

divinethinspiration says:
i like that. can i ask a question?

bodaciousbod says:
that's what we're here for!

divinethinspiration says:
anyone here have their period stop for no reason?

bodaciousbod says:
i have. it's so cool not to have to do the whole
tampon crap. i haven't had one in six months!

nevertoothin says:
i'm going on two years. my mom hasn't even figured
it out yet. i just keep flushing the tampons down
the toilet once a month.

lookingforlight says:
i still have mine. i kind of envy you guys but
i worry a little about what it's doing though,
sometimes. i mean, don't you need it to be a mom
someday?

nevertoothin says:
my doctor found out and told me that my body was
confused because it wasn't getting enough fuel
to grow properly and so it thought i was a little
kid again and stopped my period. omg, they blame
everything on being thin! unbelievable!

I stopped reading and sat back for a minute. Was it possible that dieting could actually stop the clock? Defeat Time?
Make my body think it wasn't old enough for all of the fuss
and mess and worry?

I remember my first period like it was yesterday. Actually it kind of reminded me of that whole pants-peeing incident on the trike. I felt just as gross and uncomfortable, and scared, that first time I went to the bathroom and saw the mess of my panties. I knew what it was, of course. We had learned all about it in health class, girls talked about it all the time, and there was a commercial on TV about it every thirty seconds. My mom hadn't really talked to me about it much but I knew she had supplies in the bathroom cupboard. At least I thought she did. I kind of wadded up some toilet paper and put it in my pants before pulling them up and started digging through the closet, hoping that the package would have directions. I thought about asking my mom to come in and help but I wasn't sure if she would really want to. It was kind of gross, and it's not like I was a baby or anything and needed my diaper changed. Although those pads on TV looked kind of like diapers, only smaller, and those other things just looked like instruments of torture. I didn't have to worry about which one she had in there though, because I couldn't find anything at all. This left me with no choice. I took a deep breath and went to find Mom.

"Mom?" I called, not very loudly.

"Yes?" she answered from right behind me, making me jump.

"Um, I need some supplies," I said in code. I don't know why.

"Supplies??"

"Women's supplies. My period seems to have started." I shrugged my shoulders. I felt kind of like I should apologize. I don't know why.

"Oh. I see. Well. I guess you're growing up." She seemed a little distracted as she started looking through the cupboards I had already messed up.

"There isn't anything there," I said helpfully.

"I see that," she answered, turning away from the cupboard and looking at her watch. "I'm sorry, Maddie, but I have to leave for work now. I'm already running late."

"What am I supposed to do?" I asked, trying not to whine. A girl in the process of turning into a woman shouldn't really be whining. But why did becoming a woman have to be so messy and complicated?

"Well, you can just run down to the drugstore and buy some pads. Slim fit because you're so young, I think."

"I don't know how to buy them! I don't know what aisle they're in or what to call them or how much they cost or anything!" I kind of yelled in a panic.

"Well, you can wait until your dad gets home and ask him to go for you."

"Dad can't do it!" I don't know why I said that either but it just didn't seem like a very dad-like thing. At least not for my dad.

"Then you'll have to wait until I get home or go yourself. It is a perfectly natural part of growing up, and no one will think anything of it. It's no different than buying tissues or toilet paper. Just take a twenty out of my purse. You'll be fine."

I decided not to point out that I didn't usually buy either of those things either. I could feel the panic building.

"Fine," I repeated in my best sulky three-year-old voice. Why do we say "fine" when we mean the exact opposite? We should say "not fine." I stomped off to get her purse, grabbed a twenty, and shoved it in my pocket.

We live in a suburb on the edge of the city. It's kind of like a small town around there. Everyone goes to the same drugstore and grocery store when they need something. I always see someone I know when I go out. There were much larger stores right downtown where no one would know me but it was too far away to bike to and still be home for supper.

After the world's most disgusting ride, with toilet paper bunching up into unmentionable places, I parked my bike at the rack in front of the store, defiantly not locking it. If it got stolen, I was planning on blaming my mother. I wandered into the store, trying to look like I was just browsing. I stopped at the cosmetics aisle, even though I never wore makeup. I tried on lipstick and perfume samples for a while and wondered why people bother to put this stuff on every day. I then wandered down the hair section and thought about dyeing my hair just because it would bug my mother. I moved to school supplies and wondered whether or not I needed a new binder. I contemplated the candy. I read the back of several romance novels featuring beautiful heroines. I bet they never had to shop for their own supplies! I read a few pain reliever packages, figuring that I might need some in the next five minutes or so. I even looked at toilet paper and tissues for a minute, to build my courage up a little.

Then I ran out of aisles. I looked up and there, right next to the diapers, was my target section with the quaint heading "Feminine Hygiene." Like we're dirty or something. Looking up and down the shelves, I realized that I had never actually appreciated the startling array of possibilities before. Why do there have to be twenty-seven different varieties? I couldn't for the life of me remember what color the package my mom usually bought was, let alone the brand name! Pink, blue, green, orange, yellow, fuchsia, purple! Thick, thin, slim, long, short, day, night, gel lining, with tabs, without tabs, with wings, without wings! Why do they have to call them wings? Butterflies have wings. Birds have wings. Angels, fairies, and the occasional dragon have wings, not feminine hygiene products! Do they want us to believe these things are really the objects of dreams and fantasies? Nightmares, maybe.

"Can I help you with anything?"

The words echoed throughout the store as if they had been broadcast over the PA system. I looked up to find Angela Stanton smiling sweetly at me. Of course, I knew her. She used to go to my school, and her sister was still in my class.

"No, I'm OK."

"You seem a little confused. Let me get someone over here to help you. This isn't my section."

"No, please, I'm fine. I don't need any help," I stammered, but she had already gone off to announce to the entire staff that I had started my period and was standing like a dweeb in the feminine hygiene aisle. Before she actually made it to the microphone, I grabbed the nearest package – ultra thick, extra long, with wings. Good, maybe I could fly home. I ran blindly down the aisle to the cash, threw my money down, and headed out of the store. I didn't even wait for my change.

I pedaled home with the package hidden under my shirt like a shoplifter. About halfway there I changed directions and headed for Annie's house, even though, as far as I knew, none of my friends had started yet. I guess they were going to wait until they were older than the ripe old age of twelve. Well, technically eleven, as I was about a month away from my birthday. But even though I knew Annie hadn't started hers, I needed someone to help me figure out how to get myself fixed up so that I wasn't walking around feeling like everyone knew my secret. Have a happy period? Not likely.

bodaciousbod says:
u there dt? you having period blues?

divinethinspiration says:
no period for a while. maybe not blues after all.
not so scary if i'm not the only one.

nevertoothin says:
everything's better when you have your girls. the
gws.

bodaciousbod says:
totally.

lookingforlight says:
so glad you came on board, dt. hope you come every
day. good to have new blood! ☺

divinethinspiration says:
i'm glad too. i'll try to come. gtr. school
tomorrow. sucks

```
bodaciousbod says:
me too. g night.

lookingforlight says:
sleep tight

nevertoothin says:
don't let the bed bugs bite. hah. ttfn.
```

I turned off my computer and sat looking at the blank screen for a moment. I felt like I could almost see their faces in the screen. The girls without shadows. The GWS. Like a club. And now I was a member. I wondered about all of that period-stopping stuff. It can't be that rare if two out of three of the girls had it happen. I spent a little time searching the web to see if there was some medical stuff on the issue. Like everything, there were conflicting views depending on whose article you read. I decided I didn't really care why it stopped. I was glad it stopped. I didn't like it anyway. I hated getting all bloated every month, feeling like an overgrown balloon that was too heavy to float. I was thrilled that I could feel normal all of the time. What did I care about babies somewhere down the line? I was years away from that and most likely everything would start working if I ever decided I wanted to do the baby thing. Besides, I was pretty sure I didn't ever want to do the baby thing. I mean, babies make you fat. They stretch your belly to enormously grotesque proportions and make horrible marks on your skin. It is so not worth it! Not that I need to worry about babies. As I understand it, I will have to have at least one boyfriend first.

May 1

So this is where I'm supposed to say that going to group made me see the light and I found my soul mates or sisterhood or whatever you want to call it and decided to embrace the cure and live happily ever after. That would be pretty, wouldn't it? But that sort of thing only happens in sappy teen novels and bad movies. In my version of real life, the group thing didn't really change much for me, although I have to admit that some of what the girls said kind of struck home with me. Some of it I had actually felt myself and some of it reminded me of things people had written on the girlswithoutshadows chat page. It made me wonder again for a second if it might feel OK to actually talk to my fellow "guests" here the next time I was sitting in the sunroom thinking about lemonade and boys. Although it's kind of strange hearing your own thoughts echoed like that. I mean, it really takes away from the whole "I'm an individual" thing. Of course, if we were all really individuals with unique thoughts and feelings, the pseudo–health professionals wouldn't be able to take a bunch of personal emotions and lump them all together into the definition of a disorder. If there weren't any disorders, the people who own this fancy clinic couldn't persuade innocent, gullible parents that their children had something life-threatening that could only be cured by spending gazillions of dollars in a place that was so cheap it wouldn't even let me have the Internet.

I wonder how much this place does cost? Where are my parents getting the money? I don't think they're exactly among the über-rich. I've heard them worrying about paying for university and stuff like that. Steve works part time all year and full time in the summer to help pay his way through. He even lives at home to save on rent and food and things like that. He's going to be some kind of engineer or something equally guy-like. Not that I buy into the whole gender-specific thing. I mean, I totally know that girls can do everything guys can – and a few things they can't. My grandma gave me this whole speech one day about how lucky girls of my generation are and how great we have it because we can have it all, career and kids. I suppose guys kind of have the same options these days too, even maternity leave without having to give birth first. Once guys have to have periods, PMS, babies, and stretch marks, the world will be a much fairer place. Anyway, I guess we all can choose to be whatever we want to be. The problem is that I don't know what I want to be when I grow up. I don't even want to think about it. I'm having enough trouble just surviving being a teenager long enough to actually make it to being grown-up. People keep asking me what I want to "do." Right now all I want to do is get through high school...which is going to be pretty hard if they don't let me out of here.

I am going to be so far behind. I can't believe they took me out of school for this. All my life, my parents have given me the big "school is important" speech. You know the one. School is the key to your future. A good education will get you the job you want. A good education will teach you to think out-side of the box and become a full contributor to society. Blah, blah, blah. So they shoot me the lines for seventeen years and then decide that it's OK to pull me out of school before I can even finish grade eleven. That means I'll have to finish grade eleven in grade twelve, and then I won't be able to graduate with my own age group and will have to come back and do a victory lap. Victory lap. That's what they call it when a kid has to stay in school for five years instead of four. I have trouble seeing the victory in that. It's more of a loser lap, which I now have to do because of my parents. I don't want to go to school by myself when everyone I grew up with moves on! I mean, even if I'm not exactly friends with any of them anymore, it's still better than having all the younger kids know I couldn't get through school like a normal person.

All through school, Annie and I used to talk about going to university together. I never thought it would happen any other way. We even had the school picked out. Growing up doesn't ever seem to turn out the way you plan it.

I don't know if there is any GWS left because I'm not allowed to talk to them anymore. I mean, what if they found some other group to join and I can't find them or something? Then I'd be lost and on my own for real.

Marina is cool, though, and funny. I shouldn't admit it but it's especially funny when she bugs Wolf. I think I'm kind of pissed that he ditched me at group. Not that we were on a date or anything, but he did sit with me and then leave me alone. Typical guy. Typical guy reaction to me, anyway.

Maybe Marina and I should make our own group. We can plot the demise of this "guesthouse" and draw up a plan for world domination.

chapter 14

I wasn't actually looking for a boyfriend. I didn't have a lot of time. Keeping my weight under control took up a lot of it. I had to study my calorie books and websites, I had to chat with my girls to learn new ways to get my weight down, and then I had to work on the new ways until I got them right. Somewhere in there, I had to fit in my schoolwork and spend enough time with my parents to keep them off my case.

I didn't have to fit Annie in so much though. After the whole Taylor fiasco, I didn't know what to do. I was so mad at her, I didn't know how to talk to her. So, at first I just didn't. I made sure I headed for school a little later than usual so we didn't accidentally meet up on the way. I left school right after the afternoon bell rang so I wouldn't bump into her on the front steps. I was acting like a reverse stalker and it started to feel silly. By the time we could almost smell the summer, I gave up and starting heading for school at my usual time, telling myself that I wasn't exactly looking for her but if I happened to bump into her I might try saying hello.

We did 'bump' into each other and I did say hello. It was awkward at first. We both carefully avoided talking about anything to do with Taylor or weight or computers. We stuck with homework and other unimportant topics. We slid into a new kind of relationship, sort of a friendship without the fun or the trust or the understanding. We walked to school and back together when the timing worked and talked a bit in the halls. She came over once in a while, but never stayed long, and called me once or twice. I don't remember if I bothered trying to call her or go over to her place. Probably not. I was pretty busy, after all.

I didn't make much effort to see the other girls either. I didn't really have time for anyone outside of school with all of the other things I had to focus on. I talked to them online sometimes, but I honestly couldn't find very much to say. I didn't run and hide or anything when I saw them at school, but I didn't try to find them either. I was busy at lunch, trying to get caught up on schoolwork I hadn't done at night, so I wasn't in the cafeteria very often. When I did make it in, I usually sat with Suzanne Albright and co. I still didn't have much to say to them either but they didn't seem to care. I guess I was a bit like a table decoration, an extra groupie to make sure that SA's popularity quotient stayed high. I didn't go to any more parties though. She did invite me once or twice but my waist wasn't ready. I didn't tell her that though. I came up with some other pathetic excuse that she didn't really care about.

It was tough keeping my parents off my case. They had obviously been talking to each other and had maybe even done some research on the Internet on the sites that warped your perspective, because they were trying all sorts of ways to get me to eat. They thought they were being subtle and clever, but they were pathetically obvious.

My dad was the worst and the hardest to deal with. I mean, he was such a quiet guy most of the time, and I didn't want to upset him when he tried to do things for me but his new trick was a problem. He started bringing me little treats and then standing there with this puppy-dog look on his face waiting for me to eat them. I didn't want to upset him and then have him go to Mom and upset her so I ate them. He would look so happy when I did it that I felt OK about it for a minute or two.

But only for a minute or two. Once he backed off and left me alone, I would start to feel the panic. I mean, that stupid brownie was inside me! All that fat and sugar just itching to get into my fat cells and bloat me up. I could actually see my stomach growing right before my eyes. I had to do something. I couldn't leave it in there!

The first couple of times, I tried exercising it away. I looked up the calorie count and tried to figure out exactly how much I had to do to burn it off. A couple of weeks after the party, I had finally managed to spend a little time with Devon running on the track and learning how to pace myself so I could run farther and burn more calories. Not that I told Devon that was the reason I needed to run. Someone that amazingly tall, naturally thin, and totally athletic wouldn't have understood me any more than Annie. Actually, I only ran with her once or twice, and then I started running on the treadmill at home instead because it was just easier. Either way, running calories away took time, and when I didn't have enough of that, the fat and sugar would actually stay in there and start to grow and multiply.

I had to do something else. I couldn't stop my dad from bringing me the treats, and there weren't enough hours in the day to exercise everything away. I didn't want to admit it right away but it seemed that the only solution was what everyone called purging. Puking. Barfing. Upchucking. Whatever you wanted to call it, it seemed kind of gross to me. But what else could I do? I didn't want to upset my dad any more than I had to and I absolutely couldn't allow my body to keep all of that garbage inside where it could fester and fatten.

The first time I finally made myself do it was after my dad had brought me one of those ice cream "Drumsticks" that were way too big to be called a stick. He sat there and watched me eat it, and I had to smile at him and say thanks. As soon as he left, I went to the bathroom and stood looking at the toilet. I didn't know if I could do it. I had read some stuff about it on the Internet and had some ideas about how to do it in my head. I looked at my hand and tried to imagine putting my fingers down my throat. I looked at my stomach and tried to imagine the ice cream staying in my gut, turning into horrible fat and ruining all of my hard work. I couldn't let that happen! The thought of it was a nightmare of major proportions that made tears come to my eyes and my throat ache. I had to do something. I had to do it fast before my body betrayed me and it was too late to get rid of it.

I closed my eyes and leaned over. I shoved my fingers down until I started to gag, the way I had read about. I could feel my stomach heaving and I stopped for a moment. I leaned my head against the toilet and took a breath. I could feel the ice cream sitting in my stomach like a plague. I had to get rid of it! I tried again. This time the gagging and heaving happened faster and suddenly the ice cream was in the water. I sat back on the floor. I felt sick and my mouth tasted awful and my throat ache had turned into a harsh throbbing. Even my eyes hurt as if I had tried to pop them out of my face. I put my hands against my closed eyes, pressing them back into place and rocking back and forth on the bathroom floor. I felt horrible. Sick and sore and slightly guilty for some unknown reason.

But the ice cream was gone. I could please my dad and still keep my body. I told myself it was worth it. Of course it was worth it. It was something I had to do. I really had no choice. Did I?

I lay down on the cool tiles and stared up at the ceiling, trying to persuade myself that I shouldn't feel like I had done something wrong. I wondered how long it was until it was time to talk to the girls and get some opinions that might help me figure out my own.

divinethinspiration says:
hi guys.

bodaciousbod says:
hey kid

nevertoothin says:
hi dt

lookingforlight says:
hey

divinethinspiration says:
i have a question again

lookingforlight says:
we might have an answer again. lol

divinethinspiration says:
do you all do the purging thing?

bodaciousbod says:
some do. not all. y?

divinethinspiration says:
tried to today for first time. grossed me out a
little but felt ok to get rid of ice cream.

nevertoothin says:
ice cream is easy. good to start with it.

divinethinspiration says:
it was hard to do.

bodaciousbod says:
gets easier for some. some can't stand it so try
other things.

divinethinspiration says:
like?

lookingforlight says:
ppl have their own thing. exercise, water diet,
laxatives.

bodaciousbod says:
hate laxatives. some do diet pills. i don't. makes
me feel weird.

lookingforlight says:
u r weird bb

bodaciousbod says:
hahahahahahahahah sooooo funny!!!!!!!!!

nevertoothin says:
yeah, well i forgot to laugh.

divinethinspiration says:
u guys are crazy

lookingforlight says:
but beautiful, right?

nevertoothin says:
totally going there. no shadows.

lookingforlight says:
just light...i'm almost where i want to be.

divinethinspiration says:
where is that?

lookingforlight says:
not a place. just a size.

nevertoothin says:
a size that feels like a place. like ur going
somewhere nice where ppl think u look good

bodaciousbod says:
everyone accepts u

divinethinspiration says:
sounds like a nice place

lookingforlight says:
totally

divinethinspiration says:
so i'm not a bad person for puking up my dad's
presents?

bodaciousbod says:
no. you aren't hurting anyone.

nevertoothin says:
none of us r hurting anyone. we just want to be
ourselves. our true selves.

bodaciousbod says:
our true blue beautiful shadow-free awesome
wonderful selves

lookingforlight says:
miss positive today!

bodaciousbod says:
it's a good day. lost 3 more pounds. almost at my
goal. break the 90.

nevertoothin says:
congrats

lookingforlight says:
double from me

divinethinspiration says:
triple from me. thx guys

lookingforlight says:
that's thx *girls* yl!

divinethinspiration says:
sorry, *girls*.

We kept on talking for hours and it was almost three when I got to bed. I knew I was going to pay for it in the morning but I didn't care. That kind of tired was worth it. I needed my friends and they were there for me. I had to be there for them, too.

Like they told me, I got better and better at it over time. It was still a little gross, but I practiced every time Dad gave me something. I even bought things sometimes just to give myself some extra practice. I got to the point where I could actually use my stomach muscles to get the heaving going without the fingers some of the time, which was a better way to go because it didn't mess up my throat as much and was quieter. I worked hard on being quiet because I obviously didn't want anyone to know. Our house has three bathrooms and I made sure to use the one furthest away from everyone any time I needed it. I ran the sink water or the shower so that no one would hear. I was really good at it and no one even suspected my secret. Or so I thought for a while.

"Madison, come out here! What are you doing?" My dad was pounding on the bathroom door one Friday evening. He had come home from work with cookies from the bakery, and I had eaten one after supper. I managed to get rid of the cookie and half my supper, which was excellent because it meant less treadmill, and I got kind of distracted and didn't hear the footsteps on the stairs in time to stop.

"Alex, what's going on?" My mom's voice joined in. I couldn't believe they were both out there. Was there no privacy in this house?

"She's doing it again! I can hear her!" Again? Had he heard me before?

"What is she doing?" Mom's voice sounded a little panicked. I sat there silently. I didn't know what to do. I was afraid to even flush.

"Throwing up! Puking her minimal guts out! Whatever you want to call it! She ate one lousy cookie I bought her and now she's in there throwing up. She thought I had gone downstairs, I guess. Madison! Come out here!" He banged on the door again. I could feel the tears forming. I couldn't come out! I wasn't finished. I had to finish. If I waited too long, it would be too hard to get it out. I leaned over, trying to be quiet.

"She's doing it again! Listen! Madison, stop it! Now!" My quiet dad was screaming like a maniac. I started crying but

I couldn't stop purging. It was his fault anyway! Why had he brought me that stupid cookie? What was he trying to do to me?

"Alex, this won't help her." My mom was trying to sound calm. "You know what the doctor said. We have to be calm. We can't turn everything into a big fight." I knew it! They had been talking to the doctor! No one respected my privacy at all!

"I know what he said! But listen to her in there. One lousy cookie!" Was my dad crying? No, dads don't cry.

"I know. I'm scared, too," Mom lowered her voice. I had stopped by now and had to turn off the water to hear them.

"Maybe we'll have to take her to the hospital or one of those private clinics. I don't know what else we can do."

"Shh. She'll hear you. Come on, honey. Just come downstairs. I'll try to talk to her tomorrow."

I sat on the bathroom floor. My eyes were leaking tears that I didn't want to cry. I didn't know if I was sad or angry or just tired. My stomach hurt but that was OK because that cookie was gone. My chest hurt though, and that wasn't OK. My heart was pounding, making the tears squirt out in rhythm, and my nose started to run. I grabbed some toilet paper and tried to stem the tide but I couldn't stop. How could my dad say something like that? How could he even think about sending me away? All I wanted was to be thin. That wasn't a crime! I had a right to control my body. I had a right to decide what stayed in it and what didn't. It was a choice, a life choice.

No one understood me in this house. I got up slowly and walked to my room. I stopped at the top of the stairs, straining to hear if the discussion was continuing, but everything seemed quiet. I went back to my room and closed my door quietly.

I sat down at the computer and took a deep breath. I could feel my insides calming down as I looked at the screen, knowing that my friends would be there soon.

May 3

Maybe all boys are just stupid. That's what Annie used to say when some guy randomly made one of us feel bad because he didn't fall madly in love with us when we decided to fall madly in love with him. She always told me that it was the guy's loss if he wasn't smart enough to recognize a good thing when he saw it. I think she actually believed it. I sometimes almost believed her, but I also couldn't help but feel that there might just be something wrong with me if no guys were interested in being around me. Over time, I started to figure out that the thing wrong with me was that they were totally turned off by the way I looked. I never said that to Annie though. She would have told me that I was full of crap, or something even ruder, and laughed at me.

When we were kids, I used to be able to say any random thing that popped into my head to Annie. We used to have these crazy conversations where we'd start off talking about homework and end up inventing a new type of car that ran on hair gel and had a blow-dryer on the dashboard. Life is less complicated when you're a kid. You don't have to worry about what you're going to be and what you are right now and how you're doing in school and whether the guys like you or whether the girls like you or whether you're good enough or pretty enough or small enough or tall enough or enough of anything to be worth something. When you're a kid, you mostly worry about what time supper is and how to get out of having a bath before bed. When you're a kid, friends don't betray you. At least that's the way I remember it.

But I'm not a kid anymore, and life just keeps on getting more and more complicated. Even in this place. I mean, here I am in freakville worrying about some guy! As if I need guy troubles on top of trying to avoid Red and the gang and their protein shakes. I should really be concentrating on getting out of this dump. On the other hand, Wolf is much cuter than anyone else in this garbage heap and it would be nice to have someone interesting to look forward to seeing sometimes. Maybe Wolf didn't ditch me because he doesn't like me. Maybe all guys really are just stupid and can't help it and need to be taught how to recognize quality when they see it. I would imagine if I asked Marina, which I am not going to do, that would be her opinion. She would likely tell me to teach him a lesson. Maybe I just won't talk to him anymore – assuming he tries to talk to me. Maybe I'll just play hard to get and make him realize what a good thing he's missing. Ha. Like anyone stuck in this place is a good thing. Then again, he's here, so maybe beggars can't be choosing, or whatever that saying is. Of course, if that's true then I'm back to being pathetic because if I can't compete with the babes in this place, I don't stand much of a chance back out in the big bad real world. I mean, they're all thin and everything, but they aren't exactly confident and classy like the popular girls in school. Not that I am either of those things either, but I hope that I might possibly be slightly more interesting than someone who doesn't seem to know how to live her own life.

"Hey."

I couldn't believe it. There I was, thinking my usual screwed-up thoughts, and Wolf shows up right in the middle of the mess! I hadn't even had a chance to figure out what I was going to do yet! I kept my head turned away from him for a moment and plastered a neutral, yet pleasant, expression on my face, hoping against hope that he wouldn't see through it and figure out that I'd been questioning his brain power. As if I had the right to question anyone's brain power when mine was so obviously lacking.

"Hi!" I said, much too loudly and much too enthusiastically. Not so good at the whole playing-hard-to-get angle.

"So, what'd you think of yesterday?" he asked.

"Yesterday?" I asked back, straining my brain to remember yesterday. The days tend to run into each other in this place and words like yesterday and tomorrow stop meaning much.

"The group session?" he reminded me.

"Oh, the group session. Yeah, well, that was OK, I guess. I mean, some of the things they said were kind of interesting. So, what happened to you?" I tried to keep the question casual, like I didn't actually care that he had left me high and dry with a bunch of strangers.

"Oh, sorry about that. I just had to be somewhere."

"Oh, that's cool. I was just making sure there wasn't anything wrong or something like that. No worries." Very smooth, if I do say so myself.

"No, nothing wrong. Just needed to see someone."
Someone? A female someone, I bet. He probably had a girl-friend who baked him fat-free cookies and brought them to him in a pretty basket every Tuesday or something.

I couldn't think of anything more to say. There was one of those pauses when the air seems so heavy with silence that it's pressing down on your head and you can't come up with anything intelligent to say. I scrambled around for a brilliant conversation starter, but nothing. I looked around the room for inspiration, but it was pretty bare.

"So." I used the conversation starter that means nothing and everything all at the same time.

"So, I guess I'll take off. Maybe see you at group tomorrow. I think it's at ten. I'll even stick around this time." He looked at me for a second and then walked away.

"Sounds like a hot date." Marina came up behind me as I stood watching Wolf walk down the hall. Even though I had decided not to ask her advice, I was glad to see her because talking to him had only added to the confusion filling my over-worked brain.

"Yeah, right."

"So are you going to group tomorrow to hang out with the Wolfman?"

"I don't know. I don't really like them much."

"Ah, but do you like him much?"

"I don't really know. My head seems to have stopped working and I have no idea what to do."

"Hey, I'm always here to help. Just call me the ward matchmaker."

"Yeah, right. You didn't even show up in time to rescue me. You're a big fat help."

"Watch your adjectives, chickie babe. Especially in this joint!"

"Sorry! I can't believe I actually used those words! I must be slipping."

"S'OK. I know you didn't mean it. You don't seem like a mean person."

"I'm not. At least I don't think I am. I guess some people might not agree."

"Oh well, everyone can't be smart and have good taste or the world would be boring. Speaking of boring, are you really going to group?"

"I don't know. Do you ever go?"

"I'm not much of a joiner, but yeah, I go. I'm on one of the group schedules. I listen, but I don't always talk. Hard to believe, isn't it?"

"Well, there really isn't much to do around here that's interesting. Even if it isn't a hot date, it's still something to do for an hour, and it might be nice to make the other circle babes a little jealous when I show up with the only guy." Not that I actually thought that could happen, but there's a first time for everything!

"Oh, so you are mean after all!" Marina laughed.

"I guess so. You'd better watch out!" I tried to sound tough and probably failed.

"Oh, I will. Anyway, I totally think you should go. You need to get to know the guy before you can figure anything out. Around here, group's as good as anything for a pseudo-date. And sometimes it can even be a little interesting if you pay attention." She kind of shrugged like it was no big deal one way or the other.

"I guess you're right." I hadn't even asked, but it seemed like good advice anyway. Besides, she might be right. It might be a little interesting to hear what the others had to say. I have to admit I was even a little curious to hear what the counselor babe might say. A little.

"Of course I am. I'm always right. Have fun tomorrow. Don't do anything I would do! You might hurt yourself!" She laughed and took off down the hall. I shook my head, which wasn't feeling quite as heavy anymore.

chapter 15

divinethinspiration says:
my parents are freaking out

nevertoothin says:
that's what parents do

lookingforlight says:
what happened?

divinethinspiration says:
caught me puking. yelled screamed. big mess

lookingforlight says:
sorry. they don't understand

nevertoothin says:
never will

bodaciousbod says:
never have.

divinethinspiration says:
it's really bad. they talked about sending me
away. some clinic thing

bodaciousbod says:
1st time they said that?

divinethinspiration says:
yes

nevertoothin says:
mine say it once a week at least. some day they'll
do it but i'll run away first

lookingforlight says:
they're just scared for us. think we have eating
disorders.

divinethinspiration says:
urs too?

bodaciousbod says:
all of us

nevertoothin says:
so much media about ed that everyone thinks
they're a dr

lookingforlight says:
everyone diagnoses us

bodaciousbod says:
only we know our own bodies. no one else

lookingforlight says:
agreed

divinethinspiration says:
that's what i always say to ppl

nevertoothin says:
but no one listens right?

lookingforlight says:
that's y we have each other

bodaciousbod says:
gws forever!

lookingforlight says:
gws for always

nevertoothin says:
gws for all eternity

divinethinspiration says:
gws for…i can't think of anything…lol

nevertoothin says:
lol x2

lookingforlight says:
x3

bodaciousbod says:
x4

lookingforlight says:
try not to worry dt.

bodaciousbod says:
they're probably just trying to scare you into
eating

nevertoothin says:
stay strong.

divinethinspiration says:
thanks again. you guys...oops girls, always bail me
out.

My parents obviously decided to leave me alone for a while because the whole "send her away" conversation didn't actually lead to anything right then. I don't know if they called the doctor or not, but they didn't confront me about anything right away. My dad even stopped bringing me the fattening treats, which meant I didn't have to purge so much, which was good, because I didn't really like it.

I was glad they had decided to leave me alone. I had enough to deal with and didn't need them on my case on top of everything else. Besides working on my body, getting to know the GWS, and trying not to flunk out of school, I was getting ready to apply for a summer job at camp. I was going to be old enough this year to be a junior lifeguard instead of a senior camper, and I had to fit lifeguard training into my schedule. I had always been a pretty strong swimmer and with all of the exercise I'd been doing I was sure that I would ace the course.

The first day started off with the typical length swim to prove that we wouldn't drown trying to get out to rescue some kid. I dove in, completely confident that I would be the best there. I started off strong and fast, pretty sure I had left everyone else behind.

"Come on, Madison, keep pushing. You're not even halfway." The voice permeated my brain a few minutes later. It was the lifeguard coach yelling at me. I could hear the words, but they were muffled by the water around my ears as I splashed my arms, trying to keep moving. Man, it was getting tough. Maybe I had started off too fast or something. The water felt like jelly, and I was having to fight my way through it. I felt like I had been swimming for hours instead of minutes.

"Madison, you're slowing way down!"

The words made it below the surface where I was trying to go faster and trying not to drown at the same time. My heart was pounding like an out-of-control drummer and my chest was starting to really hurt. I felt like I couldn't breathe and turned my head to take a gulp of air. I got a gulp of chlorine instead and found myself choking on it. I couldn't believe it but I had to get myself over to the side of the pool so that I could cough like an old smoker for what seemed like an eternity.

"Come on out. You don't seem to have much energy today. Did you forget to have breakfast?" The coach reached down to help me. I waved off her hand and dragged myself out. I was gasping so much I felt like a goldfish who had been left on the bedroom floor. I pressed one hand to my chest and walked over to the benches by the wall, trying to relax my breathing and make my legs stop trembling. I told myself to calm down and stop being stupid. After a few minutes, my chest started to feel better but then I noticed that my butt was starting to hurt. The wooden bench was so uncomfortable it seemed to be pressing directly on my bones. I shifted around a bit, but it didn't get better so I had to stand up. My legs decided to hold me up, which was good, because the coach was looking over at me. Everyone else had finished their lengths and were out of the pool. No one else looked like a ninety-year-old man two days after his death. Maybe I was getting the flu or something.

"OK, well done. Everyone come over to the side for lifesaving drills. Madison, are you ready to rejoin the group?"

"Sure," I said out loud, silently cursing her for singling me out. Then again, I guess I had already singled myself out enough. I walked over to the others. I didn't really know any of them, so no one said much to me, which was a good thing because I wasn't feeling very polite. I was still feeling pretty shaky but I decided that the best way to deal with it was to get back to work. The coach paired us off, giving us life rings. We had to take turns "drowning" so that our partner could save us. I was glad that my partner was a guy and that he had good aim. That meant I didn't have to actually start to drown before he "rescued" me. Once I was safely on shore, my partner jumped in and started thrashing around, making lots of panicky type sounds. I yelled for help and threw the ring towards him, lying on my stomach at the side of the pool so that I could pull him in without going in myself.

My aim basically sucked so I had to pull in the ring and try again. My partner was still working on his drowning technique so he didn't notice the ring right away, even though I was a lot better the second time. I was supposed to be yelling comforting things to him to get him to grab the ring, but a sharp pain distracted me. My pelvic bones were screaming at me to get up off the hard pool surface. They were grinding into the deck and I felt like I was dying instead of my partner.

"Hey, are you going to save me or not?" he finally called out. By now the ring had floated out of his reach, but I was past caring. I couldn't believe how much I was hurting and I was trying not to cry.

"Madison, are you all right?" The coach had noticed our little drama. I could feel the tears starting and hoped the coach would think it was just water.

"Madison?" She leaned down to look at me.

"I have to go now, I'm sorry! I can't do this!" I got up, more slowly than I wanted to, and ran to the changeroom. I went to the showers and stood inside the shower stall, letting the hot water pour down over me until it started to ease the aching. I couldn't figure out what was going on. I had never found swimming lessons to be particularly difficult before. I mean, I expected it to be a little tougher than doing crunches or running on my treadmill at home because I hadn't done it for a while, but it seemed to take more energy and breath than I remembered. I would get tired sometimes if I really swam hard but nothing like this. I had certainly never had trouble sitting on a stupid bench or lying on the deck. This didn't make any sense.

I came out of the stall and stood in front of a mirror, examining myself closely. I rubbed my hands over my sore bones, noticing that I could feel my sore bones quite easily.

I bet my mom and Annie would say that was part of the reason. They'd say I didn't eat enough to swim properly or some such crap. I shook my head and got dressed. I went back to the mirrors to dry my hair. I stared at myself again as my hair blew all over the place. My face was starting to look OK. My cheekbones were showing a little, and even my chin looked kind of pointy. I had managed to drop a few more pounds. That was a good thing. Maybe beautiful skinny models got sore butts too. Maybe that's what they meant when they said you pay a price for true beauty. Maybe it was worth it.

No, it was definitely worth it.

Who needed to be a lifeguard anyway?

May 4

Here's something that would be laughable if it wasn't just plain pathetic! I had trouble sleeping most of the night because I kept thinking about Wolf and the fact that we were going to be going to the group session together. As if it actually was some kind of hot date. Maybe there would be drinks and we could share a straw.

I woke up early and spent the whole morning waiting for the time to pass. Of course, because I was waiting for it to pass quickly, it had to move like molasses in January. Molasses in January? Where did that come from? I don't even know what molasses are. That must be one of my mom's brilliant and pithy little sayings that has somehow made its way into my brain. At least I didn't say it out loud in front of anyone interesting.

"Ready to go?" I turned at the sound of his voice, an idiotic grin springing onto my face. I wasn't expecting him to pick me up. Gee, I wonder if he brought me flowers?

"Oh, is it time already?" I asked with the casual air of someone who had so much to do that she didn't even notice the passing of time. I even glanced at my watch as if I had no idea of the hour. Of course, seeing as I wasn't wearing a watch, the effect was a little lost on Wolf.

"Just about," he answered.

"Then I guess we should go," I said because I couldn't think of anything more interesting to say.

I scrambled in my mind for a conversation starter. Once again, I couldn't think of anything. In fairness to me, it's not like I could talk about history class or a movie I saw last night or even the ever-faithful standby, the weather. We weren't in school, didn't go anywhere and, at the moment, weren't heading outside.

"It's nice out," Wolf said as we walked down the hall. OK, so I guess you can talk about the weather even when you aren't out in it. I looked out the window that Wolf was gesturing towards. It was indeed a beautiful day. You know the kind. When the clouds have disappeared completely and the sky is so blue you can see all the way to forever. I'd always loved that kind of day when I was a kid. It made me feel warm inside, as if I had just had a hot drink that was seeping into my soul.

"It is," I said, nodding. We walked along in silence, having exhausted the weather as a topic. Luckily it wasn't too far to the sunroom.

"Do you go outside?" he asked. There was a yard that we were allowed to use during our "down" time. Some people used it for exercise or quiet time as well. It was all enclosed by high walls like at the local prison, so we couldn't pole vault over them with a tree branch or something. They had flower beds and benches and stuff. I hadn't really gone out much. I couldn't see the point to heading outside if I couldn't go anywhere.

"Not really."

"Oh, I do sometimes. Marina's out there a lot. She has meditation time in her schedule and she's allowed to do that outside." He was still looking out the window. The sun was streaming in, sort of surrounding him. He looked like some kind of gorgeous angel, like that guy from the cream cheese commercials. I just kind of stared at him in a daze. Luckily he was looking outside while I was staring at him and didn't seem to notice. I snapped out of it and looked in the same direction. Marina was out there all right. She was sitting cross-legged on a stone bench, looking very quiet and peaceful. I wondered about the meditating thing. Was that her personal project, like my writing? I hadn't really thought much about anyone but myself since I got here. I didn't really know what her schedule was like compared to mine. I turned away from the window before she opened her eyes and saw us staring.

"Maybe I'll check out the yard today after group. I have an hour or so." I tried not to sound too hopeful but I was waiting for him to suggest that we check out the yard together.

He didn't. Sigh.

"Sounds like a good idea. Let's head in, we're going to be late." He turned from the window and headed for the sunroom. As I followed him down to the room where I was going to spend an hour listening to people talk about things I wasn't sure that I wanted to listen to, I wondered if I had just entered the hall of fame of lame excuses for spending time with a guy.

chapter 16

lookingforlight says:
maybe you just needed to warm up more.

bodaciousbod says:
u do other exercise don't u?

divinethinspiration says:
yeah i run on my treadmill and do crunches

nevertoothin says:
u run. wow. so hard

divinethinspiration says:
crunches easier

lookingforlight says:
there r lots of other jobs u can do. ur smart

divinethinspiration says:
how do u know?

lookingforlight says:
can just tell. u write good

divinethinspiration says:
really? want to be a writer some day

lookingforlight says:
cool

divinethinspiration says:
i never told anyone that before

lookingforlight says:
thx for telling me ☺

nevertoothin says:
u guys having a private conversation?

bodaciousbod says:
yeah, we think ur smart too! ☺

nevertoothin says:
i think we r all smart

bodaciousbod says:
have to be to find each other

nevertoothin says:
getting kind of sappy here

lookingforlight says:
sorry just trying to be positive

nevertoothin says:
u ok?

lookingforlight says:
kind of upset

bodaciousbod says:
sup?

lookingforlight says:
parents fighting a lot. talking big d

bodaciousbod says:
sucks

nevertoothin says:
totally

lookingforlight says:
fight over me sometimes. my fault. wish i could eat
for them but can't

bodaciousbod says:
not ur fault. some parents just shouldn't be
together.

divinethinspiration says:
all parents fight sometimes. definitely not ur
fault. couples have their own problems.

lookingforlight says:
u think?

divinethinspiration says:
yeah. kids can't make parents split. u know that
don't u? the big d is about them not u.

lookingforlight says:
i guess. made me eat chocolate though cause i felt
bad and now feel worse. don't do the purge thing.
too tired to work out.

divinethinspiration says:
it's ok. just eat less tomorrow. won't that work?

bodaciousbod says:
usually. just chill lfl. it'll be ok.

nevertoothin says:
just don't eat till tomorrow night.

lookingforlight says:
k i'll try. gtr. they're yelling again. need to
get out.

divinethinspiration says:
tc

lookingforlight says:
thx for helping me dt. ly

It felt good to have someone thank me for helping her. I
felt less useless than I had been feeling recently. I felt bad for
her though. Life was tough enough without worrying about
parents. I mean, mine were acting pretty stupid, but at least

they were solid. At least, they seemed to be.

My life wasn't feeling all that solid. My so-called friendship with the whole Suzanne brigade started to fade away pretty quickly by the end of grade ten, and by September of grade eleven, I had basically become invisible again. I didn't really care. I never ate at school anymore, and I was still having some trouble keeping up with my work so my lunches were better spent in the library anyway. Ruth, Alyssa, and Devon still said hi to me in the halls but I hadn't actually talked to any of them for a while. They had tried to call me different times over the summer and I know they waited for me to come online, but I hadn't been signing in recently. I felt kind of bad about that but the longer I avoided them, the harder it was to figure out how to start talking to any of them again. I felt like I would have to apologize or something and explain more than I wanted to. It was easier just to keep things casual. They had each other. They didn't need me anyway.

And Annie, my BFF? Well, not so much. We still got together after the summer, but it wasn't the same. I had a boring summer that's barely worth mentioning, with no camp and basically no contact with friends. Well, that's not true. I had my real friends, my GWS, which was great at nighttime but didn't keep me too amused during the day. I spent my time reading, working out, going online, and trying to avoid chores without success – but I didn't tell Annie about it. She would probably tell me it was my own fault or something lame like that. We didn't even buy each other dragons that year.

I still felt I couldn't trust her because of the Taylor thing, even after all that time had passed. I just couldn't shake it.

Friends didn't rat out friends. We still talked every once in a while and walked to school together when we were in the same place at the same time, but we were careful not to talk about anything important. It felt weird to be with her and not share things with her. I would catch myself wanting to tell her something one of the GWS said and then realize that telling her would just start another fight. We spent lots of time talking about the weather.

So, I was sitting in the library one day at school, as usual, minding my own business while trying to stay awake over a totally thrilling essay about Romeo's relationship problems, when a voice penetrated my brain and woke me up. I didn't recognize it at first because I had never actually seen Suzanne Albright in the library before. After all, there aren't any mirrors in there and you aren't supposed to talk, so she wouldn't be able to do her two favorite things.

"Hi," I overheard her saying in a syrupy sweet voice that made me want to gag.

"Hi yourself." It was the smooth, sexy voice that I had once heard calling me cute.

"So, what are you doing?" Suzanne oozed. What did she think he was doing, jogging?

"Just catching up on some work. I partied pretty hard this weekend." Everything he said sounded wise and wonderful to my pathetic little ears.

"Oh, really! Why wasn't I invited?" I could just imagine her Botox-sized lips in a three-year-old's pout that I'm sure she thought was endearing. If I had eaten that day, I would have puked.

"It was a guy thing."

"Oh, you guys and your things! Oops, I shouldn't have said that!" Oh, man, give me a break, was she giggling? Come on, Jesse, you can't really fall for that.

"Next time we'll invite you. You're a lot prettier than the rest of the crew I was with." I couldn't believe it. He was falling for it.

"Oh, go on. I'm not that pretty, am I?" Ask for compliments much?

"You are drop-dead gorgeous. Sean is a lucky man."

"Didn't you hear? Sean and I split. I'm a free agent." Oh, now she was a football player?

"Really? Well, maybe we can do something about that." This was the point where I should have stopped listening, but I didn't.

"Oh, but I heard a rumor that you had something starting with Marty."

Not Marty, Maddie! My name is Maddie – or better yet, Madison. Was she completely brain dead?

"Marty? I don't know a Marty." He paused for a moment as if thinking deep thoughts. "Oh, you mean Maddie. Why would anyone think I was starting anything with her? I haven't talked to her in months. She's a nice kid and all but she isn't really my type."

At least he remembered my name. But it seemed pretty obvious that he didn't remember our brief encounter. He certainly hadn't done three thousand instant replays of it in his mind until he could remember every sight, sound, and smell from that night. He had probably forgotten it three seconds after it happened. How pathetic was I sitting here six months later wondering if he might actually finally make a move.

I may not have been a big eater, but I was a glutton for punishment, so I stayed where I was, listening to them even though my gut felt like someone had used it for boxing practice.

"Really, well, what is your type?"

"I like tall blonds with curves." He was definitely flirting.

"Well, Maddie isn't tall, or blond, and she's just a bag of bones these days. Her name suits her 'cause she kind of looks like a floor mat. I can't believe anyone would get that skinny on purpose. She's always boasting about her stupid diets and she looks horrible." She upgraded the giggle to a full out laugh.

I didn't hear Jesse's response. They had started walking away by then and besides, my ears had filled up with a strange buzzing noise. I felt like I was going to black out or something. Suzanne's words hammered themselves into my brain, pounding at me until I had to put my head down. I actually couldn't believe that she had said those things. Even though I knew she wasn't that nice, I didn't think even she could come up with such cruel lies. I never boasted about my diet! She had asked me about it and seemed interested. I wouldn't have talked about it unless she was interested!

Now she was laughing at me? Did everyone think it was funny? Why would she say I looked skinny and then say I looked horrible? It didn't make any sense! Either I looked horrible or I looked skinny. I couldn't look both. She made skinny sound like a bad thing. My so-called skinniness is what made them all think I was worth talking to in the first place and now she's making fun of me? Was everyone just stupid? Was I?

And Jesse. Mr. Gorgeous, dream boy of my fantasy life. He was just a mean boy and deserved a mean girl. He just stood there and listened to her saying bad stuff about me and didn't say one word in my defense. What a jerk. They deserved each other. I hoped that Suzanne kept drinking her stupid calorie-filled beer every weekend until she became really fat and she and Jesse could live happily ever after in their fat little world.

This might sound a little nuts, but sometimes I felt like I was in the middle of some conspiracy where everyone wanted to make me feel bad just because I had lost some weight. Like maybe Annie had told Suzanne and Jesse to say all of those things so that I would decide that I didn't want to be skinny. I knew it was pretty unlikely because Annie didn't know either of them, but at that point I was ready to believe just about anything. I couldn't trust anyone. I was running out of people who were on my side.

When I got home that night, I went into my room and stripped down to my underwear like I did every night. I stood in front of my mirror and checked out my gut to make sure it hadn't gotten bigger. I put my arms out to the side to check for jiggling flab. I bent down and felt my legs as I flexed them in front of the mirror to make sure it was all muscle. I picked up my hand mirror and looked at my back end.

I had to admit that I wasn't as fat as I used to be, but I wasn't anywhere close to skinny. I had so much more work to do to before I deserved my online name for real. I couldn't understand what everyone was talking about. My mom, my dad, Annie, the teacher, the doctor, and now Suzanne – everyone talking about my weight, and everyone lying about it, or totally blind to the reality. It was like they were having some sort of mass hallucination, where they had all decided that I had some sort of problem, so they had to make themselves see me as too thin. Crazy, all of them.

I was the only one who could see my reflection clearly and it still covered far too much of the mirror for me to really believe that I could leave my shadows behind.

May 7
This time Wolf did stay with me through the whole group session. We sat quietly on the couch behind the circle and just listened. Marina wasn't in this group, which made sense, I guess, because she had been there longer than either of us and was probably in some kind of advanced level for people on their way out. This was probably a beginner's group for people who were still on their way to nowhere. Maybe Wolf was just going to this one to humor me. Which would be kind of nice if it were true.

No one seemed to really notice or care that we were there. Well, that's not entirely true. Big Red was in charge again and she did look over at me and smile. I'm not sure why she would smile, because we weren't exactly friendly, and I didn't exactly smile back. I didn't not smile either. I just kind of let my mouth stretch out a bit to the sides for a second. It was probably technically a grimace but at least I acknowledged her. Anyway, a couple of the girls glanced over at me and smiled too, and I actually managed to dredge up a smile back, with corners curled up and everything. One of them even gestured to an empty chair beside her, but that was going a bit too far so I just shook my head in what I hoped was a friendly way. I was a little disappointed that no one seemed all that envious of my position beside the only guy. Maybe they were just hiding it well. Or maybe they really didn't care because they knew that he wasn't really interested in me and I was the only one who didn't know.

Or maybe I was just being completely nuts and no one there was interested in me or Wolf because they had real, actual significant things to worry about.

It was a lot like the first session. The girls talked and Red just listened and made a comment or two occasionally. It didn't feel like therapy or anything. She wasn't telling them what to think or saying that the thoughts they had were wrong or right. Actually there didn't seem to be any judging going on at all. That was kind of a surprise because I thought this place was all about telling us we were doing everything wrong and had to change our lives to be decent human beings so we could be set free to become contributing members of society. I said as much to Wolf after the session as we walked back to my room.

"I don't think it's about the whole judging thing. I think they're just trying to help us figure out where the heck we are and where we're going and stuff," Wolf said.

"Why? Do they think we're lost or something? I know where am," I answered in a relatively obnoxious voice that I'm sure was very charming. He seemed to take all of this just a little too seriously. "I'm stuck in a so-called guesthouse for dieters that I can't get out of until I figure out how to prove to them that I want to gain twenty pounds and live chubbily ever after."

Wolf just kind of shook his head but he didn't laugh at my joke. Maybe the guy had no sense of humor.

"I know you haven't been here very long, but you might want to give people here a chance. I thought it was all pretty lame when I first got here. I thought it was all just about my body and weight."

"What else could it be about? That's why they put us here. At least that's why they put *me* here." Great. I was finally having a full-fledged conversation with him, on my own, and I was turning it into an argument. I didn't want to talk to him about the whole weight thing, but I guess it was the only thing we had in common after all. It occurred to me suddenly that my crush on him was pretty much a physical thing. Which was a little ironic, because our physiques were the only thing we had to talk about – and the last thing I wanted to talk about.

"I guess the body and weight stuff is what gets us in here, but after a while it starts to be about other things."

"What things?" I asked suspiciously.

"Oh, I don't know. Lots of stuff. Different for everyone." He looked a bit uncomfortable, like he had run out of things to say. That was probably good because this was really starting to feel less and less like a hot date and more and more like therapy.

"I don't want to get fat again," I blurted out before I could tell my mouth to shut.

"Me either! And I know you won't believe me, but no one here is going to force you to gain a whole bunch of weight. It isn't about gaining weight. I mean, that comes into it a little, but it isn't what it's about."

"What's it about then?" My voice sounded challenging to my own ears, and I wished I could go back to forgetting how to talk.

"Like I said, everyone's different."

"They all sounded kind of the same to me." Actually, they had all been a little different from each other but many of their stories still sounded familiar. I thought again that some of what they were saying reminded me of the GWS. So maybe everyone's different but there didn't really seem to be that many original stories out there. Maybe I wasn't as original as I thought I was either. Not so sure I liked that thought.

"I guess I'm saying that I have to figure myself out and so do you and so does everyone else in here." He made a face at his own answer, like he didn't agree with himself.

"I don't need to be here then, do I? I can figure myself out at home." Now I just sounded like a total kid. I'm sure he was really impressed. Man killer strikes again. But in my own defense, he was really sounding like he was selling something I didn't want to buy.

"I guess you just have to give yourself some time," he said, shrugging his shoulders a little and looking kind of frustrated. He obviously thought I was a total loser.

"I'm not a very big fan of time," I said in a less-than-charming tone, looking at the floor instead of his eyes. His eyes were much nicer looking than the floor but I didn't want to see what I was sure would be in them if I looked up.

"Hey," he said gently, his soft voice somehow lifting my chin up so that my eyes met his. I saw something there, but it wasn't what I was expecting. His eyes were kind and didn't seem to see me as stupid at all. They even kind of made me feel like they saw me as maybe almost interesting and worth talking to or something.

"Hey," I said back, because I had run out of words.

"I didn't mean to sound like I know everything. I didn't say it right. I've been here awhile and I guess I just see things different than you. It's OK. You can think what you want to think and I'm going to take off now." He turned and walked down the hall. I watched him for a minute, the way any love-sick stalker would do, then went into my room, trying not to sigh too loudly.

I stood in the middle of the floor for a minute trying to decide what to do next. If I'd been at home, I would have gone to my computer to see if anyone was online so I could talk to them about this newest development. Not that it was much of a development. I mean, he kind of told me I didn't know what I was doing with my life and then sort of looked at me like I wasn't gross. I needed someone to tell me if I had blown it or if I was making progress, or if I even wanted to make progress, or if I was absolutely out of my mind.

I felt a pang. Just for a second, like a faint echo somewhere in my mind, I could hear Annie telling me that I was doing fine and that he would be lucky to have me. She was always on my side when it came to boys. She always told me that every boy should fall for me because I deserved it.

But Annie wasn't here. Annie wasn't really anywhere for me anymore.

My GWS would have been all supportive and understanding and full of wisdom and guidance. But they weren't really anywhere for me anymore either. Not unless I could find a connected computer.

I sat for a minute and contemplated becoming depressed and sorry for myself, but I decided that was too boring. I'd spent too much time by myself recently, feeling like the world was a big, chaotic, and basically unfriendly place. I was getting tired of my own grumpy company. Maybe I should see if Marina was floating around anywhere. She'd probably have some words of wisdom on my pseudo-romance with the Wolfman.

I made my way down to the yard door to see if she might be outside. I had to sign out of the ward with one of the guards posted at every doorway. I suppose they weren't actually guards, but that's what they felt like to me. Anyway, once I had signed on the dotted line I was allowed to leave the enclosed hallway for the enclosed yard.

I have to admit that the yard was prettier once you were actually out in it than I had realized. I had only been there once, on the first day of my incarceration. I was given the grand tour that day, as if I was some honored guest who was choosing to be there for a holiday or something. I didn't really notice anything but the walls that time. But the strange thing was that this time the walls were barely noticeable. I mean, I could see them and everything, but they were covered with vines that kind of crept up them and softened them with colors.

There were several flower gardens scattered about, filled with bright blossoms that reminded me of Mom's garden at home. Mom's a flower fanatic. She spends hours every year creating what my dad calls a "symphony for the eyes." Every year she puts different flowers in. She never knows what they're called or how they're supposed to grow or anything, but they always seem to look just perfect. Everyone stops to look at our house when they're walking down the street. She spends all summer weeding and watering and playing around in the dirt. My mom loves beautiful things.

My mom. Looking at the bright colors in the gardens in front of me, I suddenly missed my mom.

Marina didn't seem to be out there anywhere. Actually, no one was there but me, so I decided to stick around a bit just in case she showed up. I took a deep breath and sat on one of the benches. The sun was warm on my face. I could almost feel my pale skin starting to look healthier. The flowers shifted a little in the slight wind that was blowing, and seemed to be smiling at me. I caught myself smiling back as if they were guests at a party I was hosting and I was about to make small talk. I smiled again, this time in silent laughter at myself. I didn't seem to be able to talk intelligently to any of the actual people here, but I was grinning at flowers as if they were going to be my new best friends.

The sky was an impossible shade of blue. I couldn't even think of words to describe it and I was someone who was full of words. I love words. I've been collecting them for as long as I can remember. I've always loved writing stories and poems and coming up with as many different ways to describe things as I could create. But this sky was beyond anything I had ever come up with. It was too perfect for words. It went on forever and, staring at it, I suddenly felt like I was free somehow, as if nothing could truly hold me back.

It only lasted a minute but it was a good minute. I hadn't had a lot of good minutes in the past few months, so I savored it the way you let a good chocolate bar slowly melt in your mouth.

Thinking of chocolate made me think about Wolf. Then again, just about everything made me think about Wolf. He seemed to have a really different opinion about this place than I did. That didn't make him right, though, did it? I mean, he was cute and a guy and seemed to think I was less than repulsive, but that still didn't make him right about everything.

I decided to stop thinking about him or about anyone for a moment while I sat out there in the sunshine. It felt nice, warm and quiet. Not quiet like no talking. Quiet like my insides were settling down for a moment or two. I couldn't remember the last time I had felt like that. It was like starting to breathe again after holding my breath for a long, long time.

chapter 17

divinethinspiration says:
hey

nevertoothin says:
hey urself.

divinethinspiration says:
had crap day. wish all guys were shot into space

bodaciousbod says:
hey, welcome to the club. we all do lots of
wishing like that.

nevertoothin says:
guys can be a pain for sure

lookingforlight says:
not all guys

bodaciousbod says:
u just say that cause you have a b/f

lookingforlight says:
true

nevertoothin says:
what happened dt?

divinethinspiration says:
oh, just girl meets boy girl likes boy boy doesn't
like girl boy likes different girl different girl
mean nasty and deserves to die

nevertoothin says:
nah, just deserves to be fat

bodaciousbod says:
we can cast a fat spell

nevertoothin says:
i think that's a different group of girls.
wonderful wicca or something

divinethinspiration says:
wonderful wicked wicca! lol

bodaciousbod says:
we can make her a size 14.

nevertoothin says:
speaking of size, i bought a pair of 0's today.
yay

lookingforlight says:
yeah, i wish i could be a size 0 but i'm still a
1. yuck

divinethinspiration says:
i won't tell you my size then. ud freak.

bodaciousbod says:
no way. we can help. we know lots of ways to
change size. it's all good.

nevertoothin says:
totally. everyone shares.

divinethinspiration says:
sounds awesome. not too many ppl around here share
with me. they all want me to be fat.

nevertoothin says:
been there. no one understands do they??? but we
do.

bodaciousbod says:
totally. did you check my pics?

nevertoothin says:
totally bodacious! lol. you look great. i can't
wait to look like you.

bodaciousbod says:
hey, dt, you check out the pic gallery?

divinethinspiration says:
not yet.

bodaciousbod says:
well, take a look. you can post there too.

divinethinspiration says:
no way. too fat.

lookingforlight says:
i hear that! no way u'll get me there!

bodaciousbod says:
u always say that lfl. we all know ur just shy. or
maybe ur just so gorgeous u don't want to hurt our
feelings.

lookingforlight says:
lol. hahahahahhahahahhahahahhahahah. but it's nice
u said it. thx.

nevertoothin says:
thing is we all have to remember that we stick up
for each other. no secrets. u don't have to hide
urself from us. no shadows.

lookingforlight says:
i know. just not ready. u guys all look so
wonderful though.

divinethinspiration says:
i'm with u, lfl. not ready either.

nevertoothin says:
s'ok. no pressure. just keep working on it till
you feel ready.

bodaciousbod says:
totally

divinethinspiration says:
thx guys

nevertoothin says:
if ur having trouble, check out tips link. lots of
good stuff.

divinethinspiration says:
will do. checking pics too so i can see who i'm
talking to!

lookingforlight says:
cept me!

divinethinspiration says:
cept me too. can't always even see myself these
days.

nevertoothin says:
that's cause ur still looking at your shadow
instead of the true u. give it time. some day.

divinethinspiration says:
don't like time much.

lookingforlight says:
time's ok. lets you get stuff done.

divinethinspiration says:
makes me think i didn't get enough done.

lookingforlight says:
no. should make you think that there's always
more of it and always another day to get thin and
beautiful. lol

divinethinspiration says:
good 1! lolx2. going to go check out rest of site
for a while before bed. need some sleep b4 school.

nevertoothin says:
yuck.

bodaciousbodsays:
yuckx2

lookingforlight says:
i kind of like school.

nevertoothinsays:
miss positive!

divinethinspiration says:
gnight miss positive and misses yuck & yuck.

The picture gallery was a collection of photographs that people on the site had taken of themselves and posted for everyone else to see. Some people posted before and after photos. Others just put on the after ones because they didn't want anyone to see the before ones. There were all kinds of pictures. Sometimes they were all alone and sometimes with friends or pets. None of them seemed to be with family members. Sometimes they had fancy outfits on, but lots were in bikinis so they could really show off their bods.

Bodaciousbod was there in a pair of shorts and a T-shirt that kind of looked like it was painted on. She had streaked blond, brown, and reddish hair and green eyes. She was smiling and looked happy with herself. She was really thin and definitely beautiful. I figured she was pretty happy with herself. I wondered if you got to stop dieting when you started looking that good or if you had to do it forever. I had to remember to ask her the next time we were chatting.

Nevertoothin was there too. Or I figured it had to be her because it said NTT. She had short, black curly hair and dark mysterious eyes that were all made up to look even darker and more mysterious. She had dark red lipstick on and a black slinky dress with heels. She looked like some kind of sophisticated vampire – not that I would ever say that to her! The dress clung to her and I'm pretty sure you could see her ribs through the sheer material. She really looked like she worked hard at it. She wasn't smiling in her picture, though. She had a very serious, almost angry expression, like she was daring anyone to get up in her face.

I was kind of glad lookingforlight wasn't there either. It

made me feel less like a loser and more like part of the group to know I wasn't the only shy one. She seemed like a really nice girl. Her name suited her. She seemed kind of sunshiny and nice. I wondered what she looked like and what her name was. She seemed like someone I would hang around with in real life. Not that this wasn't real life, but it would have been cool to meet all three of them live and in person and actually have people to hang around with.

I was sure that Ruth, Devon, and Alyssa had given up on me by now. I had pretty much stopped talking to any of them. That was OK. I didn't really need them anymore. Friends move on. It's all part of growing up.

As for Annie, well, even our walks to school seemed to be happening less and less often. The corner we always used to meet at was empty more often than not as time went on. Like our friendship, I guess. She seemed to be in a different place than I was and we were running out of things to talk about. We still tried to talk once in a while, but it felt strange, like we had just met for the first time and were trying to find common ground in order to have a conversation.

My GWS were my real friends now. I know that certain people would try to tell me that I couldn't call a bunch of pictures and words on a screen real but I knew different. There were real, live girls behind those words and they cared about me and thought the way I did about life. I trusted them with my secrets. I knew they were on my side.

I looked at pictures of girls from other forums and chat rooms as well. I keep saying "girls" because there weren't any boys at all on the site. I knew from my research that there were some boys who tried to get their bodies under control as well, but there didn't seem to be nearly as many as girls. I assumed boys didn't feel as pressured to watch their weight as girls. Most of the models on magazines that were shouting about diets and things were women. Most of the advertisements on TV that pushed all the diet clubs were done by actresses, not actors. Maybe men were allowed to be chubbier than women, so boys didn't worry about it as much. Maybe I didn't know anything about it because I wasn't a boy. Maybe I didn't really care because I wasn't a boy.

The girls in the photo gallery all looked a lot happier in the "after" photos than in the "before" ones, just like in all those diet ads. Everything about them was smaller except for their smiles. They all had completely flat tummies with nice sticky-outy pelvic bones. Their arms were nice and firm, with no flab. Most of them had sharp cheekbones that made their eyes look awesomely large. Their thighs and calves were pretty much the same size. My thighs were still disgustingly bigger than my calves. My cheekbones were not bad, but not as good as the pictures. My stomach was smaller than it used to be but still too round. The pictures made me realize how much work I still had to do.

I spent a little more time playing around with the site map and found all sorts of helpful things. There were diet tips and some exercises for specific body parts. The celebrity pics were there of course, but that didn't really interest me as much as the real person pics. There was this list of Forty Reasons You Need to Be Thin that I wished I could print out and pin to my wall, but my mother wasn't too great at respecting the privacy of my room so I couldn't do that. I saved it to my favorites instead.

Sighing, I finally turned off the computer. I was really tired. The day had taken a lot out of me and all I wanted to do was lie down. At the same time I felt pretty jazzed because I felt like I had finally found some friends who really understood me, and I didn't think I would be able to sleep. I had a desk full of homework to do. I sat for a minute, thinking. I looked down at my belly and then over at my desk. Taking my robe off, I put on my sweats and pulled my exercise mat out from under my bed. I lay down, staring at the ceiling. Closing my eyes, I silently apologized to the homework gods and started the first set of exercises that targeted unsightly belly fat that I had taken the risk of printing, figuring I could hide it in a book somewhere so no one would see.

May 10

"Hey." I looked up and saw Marina standing in my doorway.

"Hey," I said, stretching my arms out over my head and trying to work the kinks out of my neck. It was, like, 7:30 in the morning. Pretty early for company, although I was up and dressed already. I hadn't really slept in since I came here. Not enough to do during the day and too much time to sleep.

"You had breakfast yet?"

"Breakfast? What do you mean?" I knew what breakfast was. It's just that I wasn't really into the whole eating bit. I mean, I was taking in my minimum calorie requirement to keep them happy so they wouldn't think I was uncooperative or whatever, but I never went to the cafeteria.

"Yeah, breakfast. They do serve it down the hall, you know.

Some people actually sit together and have this thing called a meal here. You are on the group schedule now, so you really should be coming down. Keeps them happy."

"Oh, right." I actually did know that. I forgot that not everyone was in their little room, sipping protein and choking down disgusting food that was supposed to be healthy. That was just for the individualized people who were too antisocial and difficult to be with the whole gang. I guess that was changing. I wondered for a second if that meant I might be changing a little too.

"Yeah, it's kind of nice. You get to, like, chew and everything." She looked like she was kind of challenging me to say no. But I had to say no because I wasn't ready to sit in a whole room of people and talk to them about nothing and have them judge me every time I put a morsel of food in my mouth. Marina, who was apparently as psychic as Annie, seemed to read my thoughts.

"Everyone in there has been through their own problems – not that I'm saying you have a problem or anything." She smiled and held her hands out as if warding me off. "But they are all working through stuff of their own, that's why they're here. No one's watching you and no one cares if you eat or not. I thought you might just like to get out of this room for a while and see some human life. You can just have a glass of juice...or even water." I swear she could see me mentally calculating the calories in orange juice before she tacked on that last suggestion. Maybe she did it too. I took a deep breath and thought for a second. I had actually fixed myself up a little today. I had slightly less ratty sweats on and I had tried to tame my hair a little. I had shoes and socks on like a real person. Not that I was hoping to see anyone in particular or anything.

"It's OK, I'll take care of you," she said, laughing at my indecision, which was the right thing to do because it instantly made it seem like less of a big deal.

"Gee, thanks. I feel so relieved." My sarcasm, as usual, was lost on her as she just grinned and headed off down the hall, sure that I would follow. Of course, I did.

The room she took me to was across from the sunroom where the group sessions had been. I hadn't even known it was there. Well, I had probably seen it when they did the tour routine on my first day, but I wasn't paying close attention at the time because I was too busy looking for exits. It was a pretty nice room, painted a soft green that made you feel a little like spring was peeking in. There were lots of plants scattered around and a few chairs and couches, in what my mother calls earth tones, against the walls. Actually, my mom would have loved this room. There were several tables in the middle of the room. I was relieved to see that they were fairly small. I had been afraid that we all had to sit together, cafeteria style. As it turned out, Marina and I found a table with only one other person at it. There was a longer table over by one wall that had a bunch of food on it. I didn't go over but I could kind of see plates of different things, like eggs, fruit, something that looked like toast, and jugs of juice.

I tried not to stare at the other girls eating but I managed a few glances. I say other girls, because Wolf wasn't anywhere in sight. I felt a twinge of something – like a combination of disappointment and relief. I wasn't so sure I could really keep him interested in me in a room this full of girls and I wasn't really ready to find that out!

"So, I'm going to grab some food. You want me to get you a drink?" Marina asked. She seemed to know that I wasn't ready to look at all that food. I nodded gratefully. I figured I could just sip really, really slow so I wouldn't look like a total dweeb sitting there with nothing in front of me.

"So, hi. I'm Sherry." The girl at the table was smiling shyly at me. She was pretty, with long brown hair and big green eyes. I didn't think she looked particularly sick either. Then again, no one in here looked all that off to me. Everyone was pretty slim and all, but so what?

"I'm Madison."

"That's a pretty name. I love your hair. Mine is always so straight and won't keep a curl at all."

"Oh, thanks. I always wanted straight hair. I can only remember one time a bunch of girls managed to straighten it for me and it stayed that way for about three minutes." We both laughed, much to my astonishment. I was having a normal conversation! About hair! In this place!

"I see you two have met." Marina sat down with a plate of what looked like scrambled eggs and some melon pieces. She put a small glass of orange juice in front of me. I looked at Sherry to see if she would notice that I wasn't eating but she didn't seem too worried about me.

"Yes, I was just telling Madison that I love her curly hair," Sherry said graciously.

"Yeah? I never noticed. It's very lovely, Madison," Marina said, just slightly emphasizing my full name. I stuck my tongue out at her.

"Well, it was very nice meeting you, Madison, but I have to go. I hope I see you around sometimes. It can get kind of lonely around here."

"Sure. I'll see you," I answered. I looked at Marina. "You seem to chase people away on a regular basis."

"Yeah, it's one of my many gifts."

"Sherry seemed pretty nice and normal."

Marina raised her eyebrows at me as she ate some eggs. "Most of us are pretty nice and normal." I tried not to stare at her while she chewed. I wondered if she was counting the calories in every bite like I did or if she did things differently than me. I didn't ask, because I'm pretty sure she wouldn't answer me anyway. I took a small sip of my juice.

"I'm sorry. I didn't mean to sound all judgmental. I just meant that, well, they put us all here for a reason."

"Rumor has it that not everyone got "put" here. Some people actually volunteered to be here."

"Did *you* come here on purpose?"

"I didn't say that. I'm just saying that some people are looking for the help. Some people figure they're lucky to get into a private place like this. Not everyone can and there aren't too many free treatment centers around, so there are big waiting lists."

"You're kidding me. People are lining up to get in these places?" That was like lining up to get into the morgue!

"Not exactly lining up. But eating disorders are a big

problem these days and more people are realizing that they want to get some help."

I looked at her in total astonishment. "You think you have an eating disorder?" Marina was so cool and sure of herself. I'm not sure what I thought she was doing here but it hadn't really occurred to me that she had a reason of her own – *the* reason. Of course, not much had occurred to me because I hadn't really thought about it. I'd been too wrapped up in me. Not cool. Might be time to think outside of my own little box.

"Well, this would be kind of a stupid place to hang out if I didn't. Anyway, I've got to go. Talk to you later." She took her plates over to a table that had bins on it for dirty dishes. She had a habit of walking away just when things were getting interesting. I thought about following her just to see where she went, but I suspected that she would catch me in that act and blow me off for life.

As I put my lone little glass into the bins, I realized that I had forgotten to talk to her about Wolf. I guess I was going to have to figure out this one by myself. Unless I could figure out a way to get to the Internet, which I hadn't managed to do yet. I wondered for the millionth time what the girls were thinking about me and whether they had given up on me or not.

chapter 18

After the whole Suzanne-and-Jesse-in-the-library fiasco, I basically swore off people at school. I couldn't be bothered playing
the game anymore. It made me tired. Actually, if I was being
honest, most things made me tired. I had to make myself do
my exercises. I worked out first thing every morning and then
again just before bed. I had to be quiet about it, because, as
unbelievable as this may sound, my parents didn't seem to
approve of me working out. It was bad enough that they were
all bent about my eating habits, but they started making little
comments about my exercising too. Not like a big argument
deal or anything. More like, "Do you really need to do quite so
many crunches, dear?" It irritated me, so I just started working out in my room or down in the basement if no one was
there. I ran late at night so no one would bug me. I could not
figure these people out at all. Most parents were all moaning
and groaning because their kids spent all of their time in front
of the TV or computer and were getting obese and stuff. My
parents had it made with me, and they still complained. Maybe

part of being a parent is needing to have something to gripe about so that you fit in with the other parents. Just like being in high school. Maybe people never stopped having to find ways to fit in.

So, I just kept to myself at home and mostly kept to myself at school. Annie and I weren't exactly talking but we weren't completely not talking either.

By midterm, I had my life into a pretty solid pattern. I got up, worked out, went to school, tried to concentrate and get some work done, spent lunch in the library, went to classes, tried to concentrate, went home, ate some supper to keep my family happy, did some homework to keep my teachers happy, worked out to keep my body happy, went on the computer and chatted with my real friends to keep me happy, then did one last workout and crashed. Got up the next day and did it all again. It worked fine for me and I didn't see any problems with it. That is, until midterm reports came out.

"Maddie, what are you doing? You have to get that signed!" It was Annie's voice, and she sounded kind of shocked. I didn't know why. All I was doing was ripping up my report card and throwing it piece by piece into the garbage can outside the front doors of the school.

"No one is going to see this. Garbage goes where it belongs. In the garbage can." I threw the last few pieces and wiped my hands as if the paper had made them dirty. My breathing felt heavy, as if I had just run ten times around the track.

"What's wrong?" Annie asked. She really sounded worried, which was weird because we weren't really everyday friends anymore.

"Not that you probably actually care, but what's wrong is that I got a seventy-three average. Seventy-freaking-three!" I stomped down the steps so she wouldn't see that my stupid eyes were tearing up. She followed me, though, almost running to catch up.

"Maddie, there's nothing wrong with a seventy-three. Lots of people would be perfectly happy with it."

"Yeah, well, I'm not lots of people. I've never got anything less than eighty before, as you well know. I can't believe this happened to me!"

"It didn't just happen. You've had a rough term. You've been tired and..."

"What do you know about my term? You've barely talked to me. It's like you think I did something wrong when you're the one who talked behind my back to Taylor!"

"Maddie, that happened last year. It's history."

"If it's history, why are you avoiding me now? And don't say you're not because you are."

"OK, you're right. I have been avoiding you, but no more than you have been doing it to me. I do stay away from you these days. It's too hard to be with you even if you did want me around, which you don't. I get upset when I'm around you and I don't want to fight with you, so I just stay away."

"You get upset, do you? Why, I'd like to know? I didn't do anything to you. Is this all because I hung out with Suzanne for a while last year?"

"No, it's nothing to do with Suzanne or anyone else. It's you, Madison. I can't stand to watch you do this anymore."

"Do what?"

"This. What you're doing right now. Freaking out about some stupid report card and not figuring out that your marks are dropping because you're exhausted all of the time. Starving yourself until you look like you're dying. Whenever I do talk to you, all you talk about is food and weight and then you don't eat anything at all and you just keep getting worse and worse!" Annie put her hand over her mouth as if she wanted to stop any more words from spewing out.

"Getting worse. What do you mean worse? Worse than what?" I really wanted to hear this.

"Just stop it, Madison!" Not-so-cool Annie was yelling now. I couldn't believe my ears. What was her problem?

"Stop what?" I yelled back, just because I felt like it.

"Can't you see what you're doing? Can't you see how you're hurting yourself? Or if you don't care about yourself, can't you try to see how you're hurting me and your parents and everyone else who cares about you? Or are you so wrapped up in your selfish obsession with your skinny body that you don't care who else you hurt?"

"Selfish? How am I selfish? I never did anything to anyone!" I couldn't believe her! Who did she think she was, anyway?

"You really believe that, don't you?" Annie's voice was quiet again but she sounded like she was going to cry. I didn't care if she cried or not. She didn't have any right to criticize me. She looked at me and wiped at her eyes. "You really don't see it. You can't see that your mom and dad are worried sick about you and that everyone at school looks at you and wonders what's going to happen to you. You can't see that my heart feels sick every time I look at you and see you get thinner and more distant and less happy. You just don't see. And I don't know how to help you. I care about you, Maddie. I want to be your friend. I thought we were the forever kind, like two dragons, you know? But I can't do it. I can't hang around and watch you do this. I can't. I just can't."

I watched her run away. I knew she was crying, but I told myself it was her own fault and willed myself not to cry along with her. If she wanted to stay completely out of my life, that was fine with me. It's not like we were still real friends anyway. There was nothing to miss, no one to miss.

She was wrong. I could see everything just fine. I could see that no one really cared about me at all. They were all too worried about themselves to try to understand the things that were important to me. It didn't matter. I was fine. I could take care of myself. So much for "alwaysannie."

That night I didn't turn my computer on at eleven. I didn't want to talk to anyone. I just crawled into bed and pulled the covers up over my head, hoping for sleep to wipe out the day the dragons went away for good.

May 12
"Hey."

I was sitting by the window, watching Marina meditating in the garden and wondering whether I should go out and bug her or not. Now that I was going to group, I had a full hour of down time after each session. Wolf sat beside me and watched her for a second.

"She's probably going home next month. Did she tell you that?"

"No. She doesn't really talk about herself much." I looked at him. "Does she talk to you?"

"Not really. Mostly she just picks on me. She was here before me, though, and I'm pretty sure she's on her way out."

"What about you?" I tried not to sound like it mattered. I'm not actually sure if it did anymore or not. I'm not sure I have the energy to worry about boys these days. All this writing of my memories is making me think too much and I'm not all that happy with the thoughts. I feel turned inside out with my emotions sitting on the outside, exposed and raw.

"Oh, I'll be here a bit longer."

"Can I ask you a personal question?" It was risky, but curiosity won over common sense.

"Sure. I bet I can even guess."

"Oh, yeah? Go ahead."

"You want to know how a guy like me ended up in a place like this. Emphasis on the *guy* part." He grinned. My heart did kind of a slow roll and a couple of butterflies danced in my gut. Maybe I had a little energy for this after all.

"Yeah, that is what I want to know. There isn't much talk about guys and losing weight and all that stuff." I wasn't going to bring up the disorder thing.

"Well, here's the story. It's boring, but I've had to tell it a few times, so here goes. Try not to fall asleep."

"I'll do my best." I smiled, as prettily as I could manage. He took a deep breath and started to talk.

"I'm probably a little like you. I wanted to get my body under control. I liked control. I liked to do things well and please everyone around me. My parents weren't always the easiest people to please. My dad is kind of a macho guy, and I never was. He wasn't mean or anything, just...disappointed in me, I guess. He thought I was soft. I tried to do some of the stuff he wanted, like sports, but I wasn't big enough for football or fast enough for soccer. I liked swimming but he didn't think it was a real sport. Anyway, it wasn't that big a deal but it bothered me. I started trying to get my body into shape so at least I would look more athletic or whatever. I started getting thinner and more buff and people started to notice. At first it was all good. Even my dad said I looked like I had been working out. After a while, I just couldn't stop. I couldn't make myself eat and couldn't seem to make myself stop exercising. I swam and walked and started jogging and running. I was tired all the time but did it anyway. I found some stuff online about this diet supplement that would speed things up. You could buy it right online so I did. It worked so I took more and more of it."

"What did your family do?" I interrupted.

"At first, no one thought there was anything too wrong. No one thought of the whole eating disorder thing because I'm a guy, and mostly girls are the ones people worry about. By the time my mom started to panic, I was pretty far gone. She found out about this place from a friend and persuaded my dad to help her send me here. He didn't want to at first. Thought it was 'unmanly,' I guess. Anyway, they took me in here. I hated it at first, just like you. And it didn't help that I was the only guy around. But after a while I started realizing that I needed some help to get myself OK. I had to admit it."

"Admit what?" I asked, even though I knew.

"I told you before, when we first met. I'm sick with an eating disorder. Anorexia nervosa. Not enough food, too much exercise, and all those diet pills made me too weak. The doctors said that it could make my internal organs work so hard to keep me alive that they could start to shut down."

"Sounds a little extreme. I mean, I know they say people die from starvation but not people like us. The real sick people are in hospitals. We're fine."

"Yeah, well, I think I just missed being one of those hospital people. Lots of us here just missed it. That's kind of why we're here."

"Not me, though. I'm nothing like that. I mean, I do admit I could have done some stuff differently now that I really think about it, which I do way too much in this place. But I was never in any danger. People just overreacted. I'm not sick so much as a bit of a jerk when it comes to people."

"You seem pretty nice to me." I know it wasn't really a declaration of undying love, but I'm pretty sure I heard bells ringing and birds chirping and saw a rainbow spring out over his head. I tried not to blush or bite my tongue in half.

"Thanks. Not so sure it's true but it's nice you think so."

"Are you going to sit here all day sucking in the stale so-called air in this place and staring at the sky, or are you coming outside to breathe a little of the real stuff? You remember fresh air, don't you?" The queen of interruptions had come in without us noticing and patted us each on a cheek while smiling her devilish smile.

"Fine, fine, we'll come out. Just keep your sweaty palms

to yourself!" Wolf said, grabbing my hand and making me blush all over again as the three of us went outside to soak up some sun.

chapter 19

lookingforlight says:
we missed u last night

bodaciousbod says:
where were u? somewhere fun i hope

nevertoothin says:
were u feeding chocolate to the mean girl?

divinethinspiration says:
no. i was basically saying gbye to my former bff

lookingforlight says:
sorry

divinethinspiration says:
she doesn't want to be there for me

lookingforlight says:
u sure?

divinethinspiration says:
sure. working against me not for me. doesn't
understand

nevertoothin says:
lots of ppl don't. my b/f dumped me last year.
jerk wanted me to get help for my so-called
problem.

bodaciousbod says:
sounds like he had the problem!

nevertoothin says:
sounds like it

divinethinspiration says:
any of u lose friends?

bodaciousbod says:
some

divinethinspiration says:
what can i do?

lookingforlight says:
not much. she might come around. give it time

divinethinspiration says:
time is not my friend

lookingforlight says:
i am ur friend

bodaciousbod says:
me 2

nevertoothin says:
me 3

We talked and talked, and I realized that sometimes you have to make sacrifices for what you really want in life. After the big final fight with Annie, I didn't want to spend time with anyone, guy, girl, man, woman, or child. I just wanted to be alone with my computer where I could talk to people who thought I had something worthwhile to say. No one else seemed to be trying very hard to get me to spend time with them, so it wasn't difficult to be alone. Even my family was avoiding me. My parents seemed to have given up talking to me about anything important, which was a good thing. Even my brother seemed to find other things to do when I was home. I didn't care. I didn't need anyone bothering me. It was obvious to me that everyone had finally decided to leave me alone, which was what I wanted.

So I was pretty surprised when I woke up one morning to the sound of banging on my door and my mother's voice calling my name. I jumped awake, figuring the house had to be on fire for her to be paying so much attention to me. I ran to the door and pulled it open.

"Happy birthday, sweetie," my mom said in a sing-songy voice. My birthday? It was my birthday? How could I forget that? I couldn't believe it! All my life I had done the whole birthday countdown for about a month before. I had made sure everyone in a ten-mile radius knew my birthday was coming. I would get so excited that I would stay up half the night on my "birthday eve." Today was my birthday?

"Um, thanks?" I said weakly, as Mom grabbed me in a big hug. She was hugging me? Maybe I was asleep and this was some sort of warped dream.

"Seventeen! I can't believe it!"

"You couldn't believe that I turned fourteen either, or fifteen, or sixteen," I said, starting to wake up as my mom squeezed my ribs. Wow, that woman was strong. I tried to gently ease myself out of her grip.

"Um, Mom? Could I, like, breathe now?" I wriggled a little to make my point. Mom hung on for a second or two longer before letting go.

"Oh, sorry, honey. I just get a little emotional on birthdays. I can't help thinking about the past when you were just a wee thing, and now you're all grown up. You know, just silly old woman stuff." She kind of brushed a tear away.

"That's OK, you can't help being old," I said, trying to lighten things up a bit so she wouldn't cry. I didn't want to make her cry again. I don't know why my birthday would make her cry. It's like she didn't want me to get older or something, which totally contradicted the fact that half the time she seemed to want me to grow up instantly. Sometimes, I think that it might be nice to be a baby again and not have to think about anything but who was going to feed me and put me to bed. This growing-up routine really wasn't as thrilling as I thought it would be when I was a little kid.

"What's this about being old?" my dad said as he walked

down the hall. "Happy birthday, honey! I assume you were referring to yourself as old?" He gave me a kiss on the cheek.

"Oh, yes, of course, Dad." I gave him a kiss back and turned to go back into my room. It was so nice that they were acting all normal. Or at least an approximation of normal. It was a little like being on a TV show about very nice people. Maybe there were cameras somewhere and I was really on one of those reality shows that aren't really real at all because everyone knows they're on TV so they act completely fake. Whatever it was, it was kind of nice. Like a birthday present.

"Are you going to come down and have a birthday breakfast?" Dad asked in a casual tone. I saw Mom put her hand on his arm.

"No thanks, Dad, I'm just going to grab some juice on the way to school." I braced myself for an argument.

"OK, well, maybe later we'll have a birthday supper." He gave me another kiss and went downstairs. I swear he looked like he was going to do the birthday crying thing too. What is it with parents?

"So, sweetie, I thought and thought about just the right gift for you," Mom started to say.

"Oh, don't worry about me. I don't need anything," I interrupted. I was being very grown up. Every other year, I would have submitted my list to my parents at least two months before the big day to give them time to shop.

"Well, I came up with something. I am going to take you shopping right after school for some new clothes. It'll be a special 'girls only' time. The men will make supper for us while we're gone. We have it all worked out." She looked at me with a big smile that looked like it was going to fall off her face. The last thing on earth I wanted to do was to go shopping for clothes. I wasn't anywhere near the weight I needed to be to deserve new clothes! I opened my mouth to say it, but the look on my mother's face shut me up.

"That sounds great," I lied and was rewarded with a real smile. "I don't need much, though, just a couple of things, all right?"

"Whatever you want. It's your day," Mom said, hugging me again. She gave me another power squeeze and left me to get ready for school. That was more hugging than I usually got in a year.

We headed to the mall right after school, as promised. Our suburb didn't have anything resembling a real mall so we had to go downtown. I used to love shopping trips when I was little. It was always this big adventure, heading into the city where all of the real stores were – you know, the ones in the TV commercials. I loved it a little less over the last couple of years, but it was still interesting to look at all the new fashions. It seemed that loud colors were "in" this season, shouting at us from every rack.

I really hated the way I looked in some changeroom mirrors. The lights made me look like I had the plague and the glass made me look all lumpy and bumpy, even lumpier and bumpier than I looked at home. I couldn't figure out how the stores thought that this would help them sell stuff, but it didn't seem to be a problem. Not for them anyway. The lineups at the cash were always long and filled with obnoxious people hoping their new jeans would look better at home than they did at the store.

I tried on a couple of things to please Mom. The salesgirl was sniffing around, trying to smell a sale. I guess my mom looked rich or something. When I was there alone, no one paid any attention to me because they figured I had no cash.

Anyway, every time I would come out of the changeroom, the salesgirl would swoop down and say, "Oh, lovely, so slimming."

"If she says that word one more time, I am going to bop her in the nose," my mother said the fourth time we heard it. I looked at her in surprise. The thought of my proper mother "bopping" anyone was crazy. She looked mad enough to do it, too!

"Mom!"

"No, Madison, I am serious. There are other adjectives in the English language and she needs to learn one or two. I think we can find you something nice elsewhere!"

And so we left, much to the salesgirl's dismay. I found myself giggling a little as we walked down the mall.

"Why are you laughing?" Mom asked.

"Bop her in the nose?" I asked, laughing. Mom looked at me and grinned.

"Definitely."

We did manage to find a couple of nice things and actually had something that felt like fun doing it. I was feeling pretty good by the time we got home.

As promised, the guys had made dinner, and it wasn't too bad. Fish and rice and steamed veggies. It was almost like they knew what was moderately safe to eat or something. No one bothered me during the meal about how much food I put on my plate and we had a really nice birthday supper. I was really starting to think that there might be a camera hidden in the oven because this was all too pleasant to be true.

"Just one more thing," my dad said as we were clearing off the last of the dishes. My mom looked at him and kind of shook her head.

"Alex?" she said.

"It's a birthday, Ellen. We always have a cake on birthdays, right, Steve?" Dad smiled forcefully and looked at my brother.

"Definitely. I actually bought it for you!" Steve walked over to the fridge and took out a big, pink cake with a big Barbie doll face plastered across the middle of it. I would have laughed if I didn't feel so much like crying. When we were little kids, I was always stealing Steve's GI Joe to dance with my Barbie. It used to drive him crazy and he would steal my Barbie and put her in combat gear to help Joe win some war. It was an ongoing battle for a year or two. I was surprised he remembered, and it was kind of touching. It would have been even more touching if he had bought me something that didn't have to go into my mouth, like an actual Barbie. I mean, cake? They wanted me to eat cake? I couldn't eat cake. If I did, I would have to throw it up again. I didn't want to have to do that on my birthday.

"That's beautiful, Steve. I'll have to go find my old Barbie dolls so we can play after supper. You have a piece now and I'll have one later. I'm all full right now," I said, not making eye contact with my dad.

"But it's your birthday. You have to have some." Dad looked at me hopefully.

Usually I couldn't resist those eyes, but today they were overshadowed by the enormous piece of cake that he had put in front of me. All of that sugar and fat. A huge pink icing rose. Just the rose alone would cause me to gain a pound. What if I ate it and couldn't get rid of it later? What if it actually stayed inside me? I couldn't let it be in me, melting into fat that I couldn't fight. I didn't want to disappoint anyone, but I just couldn't do it. Why were they doing this to me? Why did they want to ruin the whole day? How could they be so incredibly selfish!

"Later, Dad, OK?" I said again, trying not to sound grumpy.

"Just a bite?" he said.

"No! I can't! Don't you get it? I can't!" I threw my fork down like a tantrumming baby and started to cry. Mom started crying too. My dad had tears in his eyes, and even Steve looked like he was going to start leaking. I ran from the kitchen and slammed my way into my room. I threw myself down on my bed and let the tears just come.

Why did they buy that stupid cake? What's so important about a stupid cake? This was my birthday. Mine! I didn't have to go and do something I didn't want to do on my own stupid birthday. It wasn't my job to make myself sick just to make everyone else happy. It was their job to make me happy. It was my birthday.

Why did Mom have to go and cry? She made everyone else upset. We had this almost completely nice day and she goes and wrecks it with her big stupid tears.

I rolled over and looked up at the ceiling. I didn't see any hidden cameras there recording my misery. Apparently everyone else was miserable too. I bet they thought it was my fault for not eating the stupid cake. I bet they thought I could give in just once and it wouldn't hurt me. They probably thought that my birthday was their day too, or something like that. They just didn't get it. They didn't understand that I couldn't let any of it into my body. I couldn't risk having it stay there and grow inside me. I just couldn't do it, no matter what anyone thought or did or felt.

I stared up at the ceiling, my tears trickling down onto the comforter. I didn't see any answers to my questions up there, which was too bad because I had one more question that I really needed an answer to.

Was there any chance that my family being upset was partly, even a little bit, my fault?

May 15
"I can get you in," Marina said. She had her eyes closed and was lying on the grass letting the sun beat down on her face. Marina had been basically making me come outside at least once a day. Sometimes Wolf came with us, but usually it was just the girls. It was good to get outside and breathe for a while. I was running out of things to write and I had started reading over some of what I had already written. Looking at my life in stark black and white had caused me to think shadowy thoughts. Thoughts that made me ask myself questions that I didn't have the answers to anymore. So I was happy to have an escape out into the sunshine with someone who

didn't much care if I shared my thoughts with her or not.

We didn't do much, but it still felt good to be out. Sometimes we talked and other times we just kind of sat there. Marina sometimes did the meditation thing but I had absolutely no idea what that was all about, so I did some drifting and dreaming and looking for Wolf while she communed with the universe or whatever it was she was doing.

Today was a talking day, and I was the one doing all of the talking. Marina and I still didn't really talk about the whole weight thing all that much. But we somehow managed to find other, more interesting things to talk about. She had told me about her parents and how her mom had been a teacher in a little village where her dad was a fisherman – which I thought was really cool because it sounded like something out of a book – and they got married and had her. She told me her dad used to take her out on the boat, but she didn't really remember much of that life because her parents split when she was really little and her mom moved her to the city and away from her early lifestyle.

"She always says it wasn't because she was ashamed of his job or anything but I'm not so sure. She certainly didn't talk much about being married to a fisherman. And we moved really far away, so I didn't get to see Dad much. I think Mom thought my dad should choose to leave that life and come and live close to us if he wanted to see me regularly. She just didn't really understand anything about it. I mean, what did she expect him to do, find a job at an aquarium or something?" She said it with a shrug like it didn't matter much to her one way or the other.

"Did you miss him?" I asked, wondering how I would feel if I couldn't ever see my dad. The thought of it made my chest tighten, which was surprising considering how much everything at home had fallen apart.

"Not really. I didn't remember much about him. You can't miss what you never had, I guess."

"So you just didn't see him?" I was kind of prying, but I was really curious.

"He came to see me a few times, but it didn't work very well for anyone. My mom wouldn't take me there. After divorcing him, she didn't want to go anywhere near the village. She didn't feel comfortable sending me on my own. I think she had some pretty narrow ideas about the kids there. She read somewhere that kids in small towns had nothing to do but get into trouble and do drugs. It's kind of funny when you think of it. She was all worried that I'd turn into someone who needed rehab – and look where I ended up. Little Marie needed to be rehabbed after all." She laughed, but not really in the way people laugh at funny things.

And that was the end of the conversation that day.

Today it was my turn to share, and for some reason I felt the need to tell her all about the GWS. Well, actually I do know the reason. I was feeling down about some of the stuff I was reading back to myself from my journal and the only people I really thought would tell me that I hadn't done anything wrong were the girls. But they weren't here so I did the next best thing, which was to talk about them. I was kind of worried while I was babbling away to Marina because I couldn't help flashing back to Annie's reaction to my online girls' group.

Marina wasn't Annie, but I still didn't know how she would react. I wasn't exactly overloaded with company in this place and now that I had some, I didn't really want to lose it.

Marina had listened to me quietly and didn't really react at all except for her comment about getting me in.

"Get me in where?" I asked.

"To the computers. Sounds like you need to talk to your friends. Let them know where you are. Make sure they know you still care about them." She sat up, shading her eyes to look at me. I should have known better than to think Marina would freak out. Nothing seemed to shake her.

"How can you do that? I didn't think anyone could get in there!" After all this time I find out I could have been connecting!

"There are actually a few of us who work down there. That's what I do for part of every day," she explained.

"You work? Why don't I work?"

"I've been here longer and I've been a relatively good girl. The work is part of the whole building self-esteem business and to help us develop skills or something. I don't know. Anyway, I work in the office answering phones and filing and stuff, and sometimes I enter data into the computer. I have the password for the one computer that doesn't have all the confidential stuff on it. It does have the Internet, though."

"How could we do it, though? I can't just come to work with you and sit there and do my thing. Besides, the only time I'm sure I can do the live chat thing is at eleven at night."

"Perfect. No one will even be on the office floor at night."

"Eleven is a little after curfew. Don't you think someone might wonder what we're doing?"

"Then I guess we'll have to be sneaky. Haven't you ever done anything sneaky before?"

"Sure, but not here."

"It's not like we're in maximum security or anything. All there is at night is one night shift worker sitting at a desk. It's not like they check on us with flashlights like in the movies."

"Oh." Actually, I kind of thought that was exactly what they did.

"We can easily sneak down, you can do your thing and we can be back in bed by midnight with no one the wiser."

"But what if we get caught? I mean, it's probably no biggie for me, 'cause I don't have any privileges anyway. But you could lose your job or something." And I could lose my only almost friend.

"Big loss. A lame job that I don't get paid for. Besides, I won't get caught. I never get caught."

"Wow. I don't know. I mean, I really, really want to but I don't know if I want you to risk it."

"I'm a big girl. I can take care of myself. But thanks for caring."

"When would we do it?"

"Whenever you're ready. Sooner is better, I think. Once you give me the go-ahead, I'll grab Wolf and we'll get started."

"Oh. Why would you be grabbing Wolf?" I kind of wanted to grab him, too, but probably in a different way than Marina did.

"We need a lookout. Planning – that's why I never get caught."

"Do you think he'll actually help us? He seems pretty serious about this place."

"I know. He's pretty uptight, isn't he? He'll do it, though. He's afraid of me and has a crush on you, so it's perfect."

"He doesn't have a crush on me!" I protested too much and too loudly.

"OK, so he doesn't have a crush on you. He's still afraid of me."

"Do you think he has a crush on me?" I was kind of stuck on that one point.

"I don't know what goes on in his mind but he seems to pay attention to you. Looks like a crush to me. What do you think?"

"I try not to."

"You do a good job."

"You're just a laugh a minute today. I mean, I try not to think too much about guys' feelings because I have enough trouble figuring out my own. Every time I like a guy, I mess everything up."

"Welcome to being a female. We all do that."

"You don't seem like you could ever mess up anything. And I know lots of girls who just seem to know exactly what to say and do around guys all of the time."

"Yeah, well, there are lots of good actors out there is all I can say. Including me. Anyway, you let me know when you're ready and I'll get things going. I have to go. See ya."

"See ya."

I went back to my room, deep in thought even though I was supposed to be trying not to think. I couldn't believe I was being handed the possibility to reconnect with the GWS. I really needed them and I knew I should be incredibly excited at the idea of talking to them again.

But the weird thing was, the thing I felt most excited about was that there was someone right here who was willing to risk her own skin to help me.

chapter 20

Things at home were kind of quiet for a while after my disastrous seventeenth birthday. No one made a huge deal of it. At least not in front of me. Everyone just went back to carefully avoiding me and working hard at not talking to me about anything I did. My parents didn't even have a fit when I told them about my report card disappearing. My mom even wrote me a note saying that I had lost it but had told her my average so that I didn't have to get a new copy. Which was kind of true except that I lied about my average. Well, what else could I do? I wasn't going to admit to a seventy-three!

It was as if we were in an uneasy truce. It was also kind of like my family thought I was some kind of bomb that would go off if anyone made a wrong move. I guess they weren't all that far off base. I felt a little like I was going to explode. As it turned out, the explosion came sooner than anyone expected, and it wasn't me who detonated the bomb.

I really didn't think things could get much worse than the day of my birthday, but I was wrong. Things could get much worse, and they did – about a week after the cake incident.

I was sitting in my room at the computer with the girls in the chat room. We were talking about my birthday.

divinethinspiration says:
i feel like a jerk.

bodaciousbod says:
no way. not ur fault. cake is evil. yr dad should
understand.

nevertoothin says:
my mom tried that last year. i ate it and then
threw up all night.

divinethinspiration says:
everyone was upset.

bodaciousbod says:
so not ur fault. u have a right to be who u want.

divinethinspiration says:
yeah. i do, dont i. i want to be thin and
beautiful.

bodaciousbod says:
everyone wants to be thin and beautiful. just not
everyone has willpower to do it. not brave enough
to do what it takes.

nevertoothin says:
anyone who says they don't want to be thin is

lying. they say we're stupid and gross for purging
but they just don't have the guts. lol

divinethinspiration says:
hahaha, that's what i always thought but i thought
maybe i was nuts.

lookingforlight says:
ur not nuts. don't put yourself down like that. ur
a good person who wouldn't want to hurt anyone on
purpose. u can't control everything around you.
it's not ur fault.

bodaciousbod says:
nah, it's your family who r nuts. mine too.

lookingforlight says:
thats not really fair either. maybe no one is
nuts. just misunderstood.

bodaciousbod says:
and that's why we call her looking for light…
always looking for the good in crazy people who
are out there trying to make us all fat with their
conspiracies and evil ways!

I often had my earphones on when I was on the computer,
listening to my downloads, so I couldn't hear if anyone called
me or even came into my room. It was never really an issue,
given that everyone pretty much stayed out of my way. I didn't
hear my mom's voice until it was right beside me.

"Madison!" Mom's voice blended with the music and

confused me for a second until she reached over and pulled the headphones off my head.

"What are you doing?" I asked, grabbing at the headphones while trying to shut down the computer at the same time.

"Don't turn it off. I want to see what you're doing." Mom actually took my arm by the wrist and moved it away from the keyboard. I shook her off and looked at her as if she had lost her mind. Dad was standing a couple of feet behind her, looking uncomfortable and upset.

"What are you doing?" I repeated, more loudly this time.

"I told you. I want to see this. I paid for the computer and I pay for the Internet service, so I guess I can look at what you're using it for until all hours of the morning," Mom said, leaning over to read the screen. I hadn't had the brains to shut off the screen even, so everything was there right in front of her. She stood there reading for a minute, shaking her head. I didn't say anything because the reality of what was happening hadn't really sunk in. It had never occurred to me that anyone knew what I was doing. I figured everyone was asleep when I was with my friends.

"What are you thinking?" she demanded, turning to look at me. Her eyes were shiny as if she had been crying again, and her face was red. She looked as angry as I'd ever seen her.

"What is the problem?" I said. "It didn't cost anything. Everyone uses the Internet. Not just me."

"It's not about money. Look at what you're doing."

"What is the problem?" I asked again. I didn't see why she was so mad. "It's a free site. It's a free world. I'm just talking to my friends."

"Madison, these sites are for girls who are sick. These things they are saying are horrible. The pictures are even worse!" Her voice seemed to be shaking.

"When did you see the pictures?" I asked, which I guess wasn't the point, but I wanted to know.

"I suspected what you were doing all night, and this morning you left your computer on, so I checked your favorites. I don't know which one you're spending all your time on, so I looked at everything. The chats, the pictures, the so-called expert information. Don't you know what this is? These are all girls with serious problems, Madison! They're starving themselves and this Internet garbage makes them think it's OK. It makes you think it's OK!" Mom stopped and sat down on my bed. She closed her eyes for minute. There were tears leaking out from under her lids.

"You went on my computer. You think my leaving it on was some kind of open invitation to invade my privacy? These girls don't have problems. They're not sick. They're just making a choice for themselves. You're the one who's sick. So paranoid that you would actually sneak into my room like that!" I couldn't believe my ears. I couldn't believe I had been so totally out of it this morning that I had actually walked out of my room leaving myself logged in. Then again, it never, ever occurred to me that my mother would take that as permission to look. It was like reading someone's diary! I mean, I never saw her as the world's greatest respecter of privacy but this was going too far, even for her. My mother had no defense here. Unreal.

"Don't make this about me. I did what any mother would do. It's my job to protect you and I'm not going to apologize for doing it. This is about you and these girls you think are so wonderful. You think these girls are talking about choice? They're making a choice? What kind of a choice is it to decide to stop eating and hurt yourself and anyone who loves you? Who would choose that?" Mom was getting pretty close to yelling, so I decided I could yell right back at her.

"I can't believe you see it that way! You're talking like they're – we're – all a bunch of monsters or something. That we don't care about anyone but ourselves!" How could she be so blind?

"I don't think any of you are monsters. You're all little girls who are trying to figure out big problems. You need to talk to real, live human beings who can help you."

"Newsflash, Mom. These are real live human beings, just like me. You don't have to see someone for them to be real. And they do help me. They're the only ones who understand me and don't think I'm stupid or something. You're just proving that even more right now. You don't get any of it at all." I felt like crying myself but I wouldn't let the tears come.

"They don't love you. I love you. I want you to be well and happy. All of these girls need someone, an adult to help them. I want to find someone to help you." Mom's voice softened. I wasn't buying the whole calm voice persuasion tactic.

"No, you just want me to be fat. You never supported my diet, ever. I had to do this all by myself. I needed to find some answers. I don't regret it at all. I found some real friends for the first time in my life."

"Why on earth would I want you to be fat? That doesn't even make sense. I just want you to be healthy. And you have always had friends, Maddie. You aren't seeing things clearly these days. You're scaring me. You're my baby. I just want to make sure you're well." Mom reached out to stroke my hair, but I pulled away from her.

"I'm not sick. I'm fine. Stop saying I'm sick. I'm fine!" I sounded like a demented parrot but I couldn't find another way to tell her. She didn't want to listen and I was tired of talking.

"Madison, I can't let you keep on talking to these girls. I can't let you be a part of it. And I don't want you going off and finding another site. We're taking the computer out of your room today. You can use the one in the living room."

"Are you kidding me? You can't do that! I'm not some little kid! You can't make me use the computer in the living room so you can spy on me! It's bad enough that you spied on me in my own room!"

"It's the only thing I can think of right now. I want to help you and you won't let me. This is the only thing I can do." Her voice sounded tired, but I didn't care.

"You aren't helping me. You're just messing everything up! This is the only thing I look forward to! These are the only people who understand me! They're the only ones who stop me from feeling like crap! You can't do this!" I felt panicky. I couldn't believe what she was saying. I didn't want to be all alone. She couldn't do it.

"I'm sorry, Madison, it's all I can do. Your dad is going to take your computer out now." Dad had been standing there quietly, like a roadie waiting for his cue from the star of the show. He stepped forward at my mother's words. He looked uncomfortable and upset, but I didn't care about him either.

"No!" I screamed it. "You have no right! This is my life! I can live it the way I want! You have no right!"

"I'm sorry, Madison. We have to start somewhere. We will get you some help. We've been talking to some people who are able to help you." My mom was still doing the talking. My dad seemed to be standing in suspended animation, like he didn't know what to do. No matter what he chose, he would totally upset one of us. Looking back, it was probably tough for him, but at the time I could only see that it was tough for me. Not just tough. Unbearable.

"I don't need help!" I yelled and jumped to my feet. I knocked the computer screen off the table where it fell to the floor and smashed. I stood a minute and looked at it. I looked at my parents. Steve came running in the door, looking frightened. He seemed wide awake and had probably been listening at the door. Another spy. He looked like he was going to say something, but my mother shook her head at him and he just stopped and stood there staring at me.

"There. Now you don't have to worry about it. It's broken. Here, let me finish it." I gave the screen a kick and then took the computer tower and smashed it on the floor before my parents had time to react.

"Madison, stop that!" My dad finally moved again, stepping forward to stop me from smashing the rest of the computer pieces, but I was done. I stood and looked at my family, my tears finally letting loose.

"Please get out. Just leave me alone. Please," I pleaded with them. I was so terribly tired. I needed to be alone. My parents looked at me for a moment. My mother turned away first and reached back for my father's hand. He looked at me again and then left with her. Steve stood there for another minute. He had the same look in his eyes that he did the day he tore all the ligaments in his knee playing soccer. He looked like he wanted to say something to me, but I guess he couldn't think of anything because he just shrugged his shoulders and left.

They all left me alone with my broken computer, random pieces of my life scattered all over the floor.

I looked at the shards of my friends and felt the floodgates open. I cried until my eyes were as dry as sandpaper and there were no more tears anywhere in my body.

When my parents came to me a couple of days later and told me that I was going to a special place in the city where nice people would help me, I didn't even argue. It didn't matter anymore. Nothing mattered anymore.

May 20

So many days of writing out my past, and I'm becoming less and less sure of who I really am. It's like looking in a mirror and being unable to recognize the face staring back at me, wondering what this stranger is really thinking about.

I thought I had this all figured out. Looking back, I was sure I knew what I was doing. I have a right to do what I want with my own body, and so I did it. I wasn't hurting anyone, including myself. I knew this absolutely. I had it confirmed by my GWS and everything. My parents and Annie were wrong and I was right. Simple.

I was in this godforsaken prison for dieters due to a lack

of understanding on my family's part. Period. Paragraph. End of the story.

But as I read some of the stuff that has happened over the past couple of years, I am starting to wonder a little if I absolutely knew what I was doing after all. Not that I think I've been totally wrong here or anything. But I'm starting to wonder a little. It's hard to put it into words, which is something pretty new for me because putting things into words is one of my best tricks.

But when I look at my own words, and read back the part about losing my best friend, I don't know what to say anymore. When I read it to myself, it's like I'm stepping back and looking at my own words through someone else's eyes. Not that I want to give her any credit, but I'm starting to think that maybe Red was on to something with the whole writing assignment.

So, the next time I sat there and started reading it, I made myself actually remember it. I thought about Annie and who she is, and who she always was to me. Then I read it again, only this time, I switched the roles. I put myself into Annie's place and put her into mine. I tried to see what Annie had seen. I tried to imagine how I would feel if I thought Annie was sick and couldn't help herself. Wouldn't I do anything I could to make it right for her? Wouldn't I tell anyone I had to that I thought there was something wrong? It's like that kid with the scars on her arms. I didn't tell and I should have. I can see that now. If it were Annie, I would tell. I would shout it from the top of the tallest building in town, which isn't very tall, but I would still do it. I would tell my mom and her mom and the teacher and the doctor and the dog down the lane if I thought it would help her. I would do what I thought I had to do to help my very best friend. Even if I was wrong in her eyes, I would still do it if I believed it was right for her. At least, I hope I would.

My very best friend. I could feel the tears welling up and decided not to fight them. I needed to cry. I had messed up. All this time, I'd been so angry and so sure that I was right and she was wrong. Now she was gone and I was here and I didn't know how to fix it. I screwed everything up! I pushed her out of my whole stupid life and all she was trying to do was help me because she thought I was in trouble.

I want to talk to someone about this. I'm all twisted up in knots and I don't know how to untie them. I'm still not sure that I want to spill my guts to a bunch of strangers in one of those circle sessions, although I have to admit that I'm not sure anymore that I *don't* want to talk to them, either. Wolf wouldn't want to listen to me whine about my stupid past, and besides, I don't really want him to know that I was a complete loser. Marina would probably listen, but I'm not so sure I want her to know what a lousy friend I've been, either. Big Red would probably be more than happy to listen, but I'm definitely not ready for that. Although there is part of me that is starting to think it might be better than nothing.

But I *do* have something. I have my GWS. They would listen, or read, I guess, and wouldn't judge. They were there for me when it happened. They would still help me with it. I know they would. I need to find them.

It's time to take Marina up on her offer. She seemed pretty

sure that it would be OK, and I guess I have to trust her on this one. I don't want her to get in trouble. I don't want me to get in trouble, either. But my need to stay out of trouble isn't as strong as my need to find my friends.

May 21
Marina was right about Wolf. He didn't seem to be all that worried about helping us and came with us to breakfast so we could plan our big adventure. Actually, to be honest, Wolf and I sat and listened to Marina plan our big adventure. She drew a floor plan for us on a paper napkin. None of our rooms were all that close to where the night shift worker sat and read her book. What exactly was she sitting there for anyway? Did they think there might be an uprising of skinny girls wielding carrot sticks in the middle of the night?

I couldn't figure out how we could be absent from our rooms for any length of time. It's not like they did a sweep every hour or anything, but you never knew when the worker might get bored and decide to do a little room inspection. Marina was confident that we could do the old pillow in the bed trick just on the very off chance someone peeked into our room, which would give us time to sneak down the hall and the stairs to the office floor below. She mapped it all out in intimate detail and made it seem so easy that Wolf and I shared a little bit of her confidence by the time we finished and headed off to attend all of our scheduled events like good little boy and girls.

My confident feelings had pretty much all floated away by nighttime as I sat in my room, sweating like a pig and trying not to shake, watching the clock tick away the minutes until our big caper. Time and its tricks. We were meeting at 10:45, and at 10:35, after about an eternity or two of waiting and sweating, I got up and shoved my pillow under the blankets, jumbling them all around to look like I was still there. I had always thought that trick looked so bogus in movies, but glancing back I had to admit that if you weren't looking too hard, you wouldn't really know that I was gone.

I slipped out into the hall like a thief in the night, plastering myself against the wall. I looked up and down, fully expecting a bright light to be shone into my eyes as I was caught in the first thirty seconds. Nothing. Not a sound. I couldn't even see the night shift worker from where I was, so I was pretty sure she couldn't see me. I slunk down with stealthy grace, my slippers making no sound as I made my way. I eased the door to the stairwell open, praying that it wouldn't creak. It answered my prayers, and I slipped through.

I ran down the stairs as fast as I could without falling, which would have ruined everything because if I broke my leg we would most likely get caught. I found the second floor, which wasn't too difficult because I had only come from the third floor. I opened the door and looked up and down that hall. You would have thought that all of those doors would be locked in a prison, but I guess this place was minimum security.

"Hi." I screamed right out loud at the sound of the voice in my ear and then clamped my hand to my mouth. Marina laughed.

"Don't worry. This is the office floor. It's been closed since five. Wolf's already down in the office waiting. Let's go."

I followed her down the hall with my hands still clamped to my mouth. I didn't trust myself and I wasn't so sure the walls were all that soundproof. Wolf was standing in the doorway of the office. He smiled at me. I took my hands away to smile back. Marina looked at us both and shook her head.

"OK, you guys, save the smile-fest for after we get this done. Wolf, you stay in the doorway but far enough back that they won't see you if they come down."

"What? Who might come down? I thought this place was dead!" I started to panic again.

"It is. You just never know what the security guard will decide to do, and I just want to take the precaution. I'm sure it's fine. Relax." Marina patted me on the head. I looked at Wolf. He just kind of shrugged his shoulders, which wasn't very reassuring, but I went in with Marina anyway. It was too late to turn back now and besides, this was for me after all.

We were standing in a small reception office that I vaguely remembered from the first day I came. I have a recollection of my parents signing my freedom away while a lady sat there in that very room and logged my life into their database. It seemed fitting somehow that I was reclaiming some of my freedom in the same place where it had been ripped away.

"How'd you get in here?" I asked. "Wasn't it locked?"

"Trade secret. Some things you're better off not knowing," she replied, sitting at the computer and booting it up. She entered the passwords and logged on to the Internet.

She stood up and gestured to the chair. I sat down and typed in the address. I looked up at her and smiled.

"Thanks. You have no idea what this means."

"I have some idea. I never did the whole computer pal thing, but I have things I miss that mean a lot. Do you want privacy?"

"No, it's OK. I wouldn't mind a little company." I surprised myself with my own answer. I had kind of expected to want to be alone to do this, but once I got there I felt like I needed someone close by.

"Girls without shadows?" Marina asked, reading over my shoulder as I brought up the chat room part of the website.

"Yeah, it's kind of like getting rid of the negative shadows of your past – you know, starting fresh with a new body and outlook and everything."

"Interesting. I kind of like shadows. They're like inverse reflections of sunlight. They tell you where you are and help you find where you're going."

I had never thought of it that way, which I was about to tell her but was distracted by the request-for-login box popping up on the screen.

I took a deep breath and typed in my login information and waited a second for the chat room to come up. I was kind of nervous. Maybe they had disbanded or found another site or met at another time.

```
nevertoothin says:
dt, is that you?

divinethinspiration says:
yeah, it's me.
```

bodaciousbod says:
omg! where've u been?

divinethinspiration says:
locked away in prison.

nevertoothin says:
clinic?

divinethinspiration says:
yeah. yuck.

bodaciousbod says:
bad?

divinethinspiration says:
really hated it at first. a little better now.

bodaciousbod says:
i hated it.

divinethinspiration says:
u????

bodaciousbod says:
year ago. stayed for three weeks then got out. not
for me.

nevertoothin says:
u'll never get me in one of those places. they
just make u pig out.

divinethinspiration says:
not really. other stuff here too.

bodaciousbod says:
we missed u. worried about u. thought maybe u
dumped us.

nevertoothin says:
yeah, but lfl said u wouldn't do that.

bodaciousbod says:
!!!

nevertoothin says:
sorry.

divinethinspiration says:
where is she anyway? taking a night off?

There was no response for several minutes. I thought maybe the powers that be had somehow figured out we were on and shut us down. Or maybe the computer just froze. I was about to ask Marina what she thought when nevertoothin came back on and sent me a link. I clicked on it and sat back watching as a full-screen image came up in front of me.

It was a picture of a young girl, maybe fourteen or fifteen. She was smiling into the camera with big brown eyes that looked gentle but somehow older than the rest of her face. Her hair was hanging over her shoulder in two braids that had yellow ribbons woven through them. She had a soft-looking yellow sweater on as well and had been photographed only from the waist up. You couldn't really see much of her body, but it was obvious that there wasn't much of one there. She was really thin, thinner than most of the girls floating around this place.

There were words written across the yellow sweater, a poem someone had added to the page. I leaned forward to read them better. As the words sunk in, I felt my stomach start to clench and my eyes start to burn. I found myself clamping both hands over my mouth. I don't know why people do that when they hear bad news. Maybe they're trying not to let it in or something. Marina must have seen my reaction, because she stood up from where she had been sitting behind me to take a closer look.

LOOKING FOR LIGHT
She always looked for the light
When others saw only shadows
She was able to feel hope
When others felt only despair
She searched for love
Never believing in hate
She gave acceptance
When others pushed her away
She tried to find perfection
In a less than perfect world
And the searching finally made her tired
And she gently slipped away
An angel flying away from the shadows
And into a ray of sun.

After another second or two, I minimized the window, and the chat page came back.

nevertoothin says:
she died about two weeks ago. right after she finally posted her first pic. she was so proud of it. now it's just her memorial pic. so sad.

bodaciousbod says:
we only found out because her sister knew about us and came on to tell us.

divinethinspiration says:
???
???
???
????????????

nevertoothin says:
they say she had heart failure. they say she had an eating disorder and it killed her.

bodaciousbod says:
i thought we vowed not to say that
again!!!!!!!!!!!!!!!!!!!!

nevertoothin says:
sorry but she deserved to know.

bodaciousbod says:
she deserves the truth. we know it isn't true. she didn't have any disorder. they just want everyone to think that so they'll shut us down.

```
divinethinspiration says:
they really think that dieting killed her?


nevertoothin says:
not just dieting but sort of, yeah. they say she
had anorexia and bulimia.


bodaciousbod says:
i'm outta here. sorry dt. can't talk about this.


nevertoothin says:
sorry dt. it's been hard. everyone's confused.
hopefully talk to you again.
```

And then they were just gone.

"I'm so sorry that you lost your friend," Marina said softly. I said nothing as I turned off the computer.

I sat still, looking at the screen as the last shreds of light disappeared into darkness. What were they talking about? Maybe I misunderstood. Did they say she died? That a little girl with yellow ribbons in her hair had a heart attack and died? A little girl who had been my friend, when not too many other people wanted to be, was gone because she didn't eat enough?

"I'm so sorry, Maddie." Wolf had come into the room, and I guess Marina had told him.

"She was just a kid," I said, letting my hands drop helplessly into my lap, my voice breaking into pieces of tears. "You saw her. Just a kid. You should have talked to her. I should have talked to her. I never even talked to her. I never even heard her voice. She seemed so smart and together and figuring her life out. She was always so positive, you know? Even when the other girls, and me, were all stupid and putting ourselves down, she was positive. She really believed in us, the GWS." I started to cry. Marina put her arm around me, but I pushed her away.

"She was my friend when I thought I didn't have any friends. She got me, you know? She was the most together one of all of us. She just wanted to look good. You know? Get rid of her stupid shadows!" I knew my voice was getting louder and that I should try to calm down, but I had to make them understand.

"Madison," Marina said, very quietly and very gently. It reminded me of that voice my mom used when I was a kid and she wanted to make me listen to her but didn't want to yell. She would always use my full name, and for some reason it always worked. It worked when Marina did it, too, and I stopped talking and looked at her. I was waiting for her to talk and say something wise and magnificent that would make sense. I wanted her to tell me how a little girl could be dead. Gone. Never coming back. I never even met her, and now I never would. I could feel my breathing getting all heavy and my heart seemed to be beating too fast. I put my hand on my chest to try to slow it down but it didn't work. I closed my eyes for a moment, trying to slow everything down. Maybe I could slow time down and make it go backwards and all of the words on the computer screen would never have been there at all.

"Madison, can you look at me?" Marina put her hand back on my shoulder and this time I let it sit there. I opened my eyes and looked at her. Her eyes were full of tears and she was kind of biting her lip as if she didn't want to let any more words out. She seemed to take a deep breath and then started to speak. I had wanted her to say something, but now I didn't want to listen to her. I didn't want to listen to anything but I couldn't stop myself. I just stood there staring at her while the world inside my head blew up.

"This eating disorder thing sucks. Sometimes it kills kids if they don't get help."

"Kids don't have heart attacks."

"Not usually, but it's like my doctor warned me," Wolf said in the same kind of gentle voice that Marina was using, like he was afraid I would shatter if he spoke too loudly. "He said my heart had already been affected and that I was lucky. That lots of kids don't figure it out until it's too late."

"But she wasn't sick." I ignored the little nagging voice of doubt that was starting at the back of my brain.

"Maybe she was. Maybe she didn't want to be or want to admit it. I don't know. I didn't know her."

"Well, I did. At least I thought I did. I don't know anymore. I don't know anything. I don't know how to feel. I have to go. I have to think or sleep or something." I ran from the room, tears streaming down my face for a friend whom I had never met. A friend whose name I didn't even know.

May 22

I closeted myself in my room and stayed up most of the night, trying to understand. I felt like my whole world had fallen apart. I couldn't even begin to get my head around it and I couldn't stop crying long enough to think. My feelings were raging around in a dark, swirling fog, confusing my mind and making my head ache and my chest feel tight.

Why did I feel this way? This was someone who was no more than words and a picture on a computer screen. Someone who didn't know my name any more than I knew hers. I didn't know anything about her, really. I didn't know where she lived or who she lived with or what school she went to or anything.

But I did know that she was sweet and positive about life and wanted the best for everyone she knew. I knew that she was kind and considerate and cared about other people. I knew that she was hurt by the ugliness in the world around her and that she hated the fighting at home. I knew that she liked me and tried to help me. Maybe knowing all that was more important than knowing her name. Do you have to see someone standing in front of you to call her your friend? Or do you just have to understand her and trust her and know that she understands you and trusts you, too?

I also knew that she hadn't seemed all that different from me in some ways. I mean, I wasn't as sweet or positive or nice as she was. I had a lot to learn from her on that score. But in other ways we were the same. She just wanted to have a little control over her life, her body. She just wanted to figure out how to feel good in a confusing mess of a world that seems to get messier the older you get.

She wasn't trying to hurt herself. She didn't have some sort of death wish. She just wanted to feel pretty and good about herself. She wasn't hurting herself, was she? She wasn't doing anything wrong, was she? Maybe this didn't have anything to do with eating or not eating. Maybe there was something else going on that no one knows about. Some people are born with heart conditions and stuff. Maybe she had been sick and just didn't want to tell us.

I had read all of that medical stuff about the things that eating problems could do to you. Heart attacks had been on the list. But I didn't believe it could actually happen in the real world to a real person. How could dieting make your heart decide to die? It just didn't make sense to me. Heart attacks come from diseases or smoking or being old and eating too much. Not from being young and eating too little.

But then there was the stuff that Wolf said about his doctor. He was only seventeen, like me, and his doctor told him his heart was already affected. Could LFL really have died from not eating enough? Did she have an eating disorder after all? None of the GWS thought they had disorders, including me. I always knew that some people had eating disorders – after all, this place was full of them. But they weren't me or my friends.

Except for Marina. And Wolf. And all the girls I met in group. I closed my eyes at the inevitable next thought so I could block it out. My head was spinning around and around and I felt like I was going nuts.

I guess I spun myself into exhaustion because I finally drifted off to sleep. I know I was asleep because all of a sudden I woke up. I sat up in bed, totally weirded out and with no idea where I was. I felt like I used to when I had a nightmare as a little kid and I had a sudden urge to see my mom. I blinked a couple of times and tried to focus. I was still half stuck in a dream.

I had been sitting in the cafeteria at school, which should have felt strange, but it didn't. I was at a table with my friends, drinking a bottle of water and just kind of chilling. Ruth was there, and Devon and Alyssa. I asked them where Annie was and they all just laughed. Devon pointed to the table next to me and made a face as if she thought I was nuts. Alyssa looked at her and laughed again and then they both started eating a great big chocolate cake. They didn't offer me any and I didn't want it anyway because I had just started a diet and was trying to lose weight. It looked good, though.

I looked over to see what Annie was doing. She was sitting at a table with two other girls. She looked different somehow. I couldn't figure it out at first, but then I realized she had finally managed to dye her hair red. It was all braided and the braids were hanging down over her shoulders. I think I laughed because I knew she would be so pleased with herself for finally managing it.

She waved at me and gestured for me to come over. I stood up and walked away from the chocolate cake pig-fest and headed over to the other table.

As I got closer, I realized that it wasn't Annie at all. The girl with the braids had the face I had just seen on the computer screen. The other girls at the table were the living, breathing versions of the pictures I had seen of nevertoothin and bodaciousbod. They were dressed in the same clothes as in the first photographs I had seen of them on the website, which I guess made some sort of weird sense. All three of them were smiling at me as if they were used to seeing me every day.

"I thought you were dead!" I said to LFL. She looked at me in surprise.

"That's a strange thing to think. If I was dead, would I be sitting here in the cafeteria? I'm just fine. Do you like my hair? Don't I look wonderful?" She stood up and started twirling around and around and around. Her yellow ribbons fluttered around her, swirling around like she was doing a bizarre rhythmic gymnastics routine.

"Where's Annie?" I asked, but no one answered. Everyone in the room got up in some sort of ghoulish choreographed movement and started twirling around and around until the whole room was a spinning mass of color and confusion.

"Where's Annie?" I shouted, but no one could hear me. "Where's Annie?"

I shouted it again and threw myself into the mass of bodies, trying to find her and calling her name. I could feel myself getting caught up in the movement and chaos, my mind spinning along with the bodies, and I just gave up and closed my eyes, sinking into oblivion, lost and scared and alone.

When I opened my eyes again, I was sitting up in bed, in a room that wasn't mine, my head still spinning. For the first time in what seemed like forever, I found myself wanting my mother and wondering where my best friend was.

I stayed in my room all day. Marina checked in on me a couple of times and so did Wolf. It was nice of them and everything, but I couldn't find anything to say to either of them.

I had run out of words.

May 25

Once my words ran dry, I mostly just sat and thought, which didn't help much because it created more questions than answers. I got so turned inside out and backwards that I was afraid I would have to spend the rest of my life alone in a room, staring at the walls, trying to figure out if I had anything to say that would make any sense.

I had individual counseling appointments scheduled every day. I didn't always have the same counselor. You could request that, but I think they tried you out on a variety pack first, so you could see if you gelled with one of them or something like that. I had never really talked in one of my sessions. I treated the counselors kind of like the doctor – the less said by me the better. I never asked questions and seldom provided answers. I had made a conscious decision not to try to figure out my subconscious, or whatever it was that I was supposed to be trying to do. I had made a decision not to try at all, I guess.

After a few days of literally wondering if my mind, conscious or unconscious, was starting to actually leave my body, I began to think that maybe I should start trying to see if someone could help me make sense of things. I was having bizarre dreams that wouldn't have been so bad if they had stuck to happening when I was asleep. But even when I was awake, strange and frightening images kept coming into my head no matter how hard I tried to make them stop. I couldn't make sense of lookingforlight's death any more than I could make sense out of my own life. I couldn't get my head around it, my words around it, or my feelings around it. I didn't even know how to start talking about it. I knew on some level that Marina and Wolf would have done anything I needed to help me, but I just felt like this was too big and too messed up to try to figure out with other people who were still trying to figure themselves out too. Without my GWS to fall back on, I felt like I really had nothing.

So, now that I actually had nothing to lose, I decided that it was time to try opening my mouth. I had no idea what was going to come out of it. I had even less idea of what anyone could say that would help. I wasn't sure if I could really go through with it, but I couldn't think of anything else to do. I didn't want to completely lose my mind and I was pretty sure that I had already misplaced it. I didn't know if anyone could help me find it, but I wasn't really doing such a good job on my own. I needed another set of eyes.

So, I took a deep breath and promised myself that the very next appointment would be the one. I would try to keep an open mind – which was tough to do since mine was missing – and dig down for a positive attitude. After all, these people were here with nothing to do but listen. I didn't even know what I needed or wanted anymore. Just...something...

Of course, when the moment finally came, it *would* have to be Big Red. I shouldn't have been surprised. She seemed to show up everywhere. I sat there for a few minutes looking at her, while she sat for a few minutes looking at me. Pretty much the same routine I was used to with any of the counselors. She was smiling in a nice way, not too big like she was about to sing a happy tune or anything, but just kind of gentle and like she had all the time in the world. Maybe she had always looked like that and I hadn't noticed before. I tried a little smile back, but my smile reflex wasn't working just yet. Maybe it was lost along with my mind. I closed my eyes for a second and sucked in a deep breath. When I let it back out, I let out some words also. Actually, once they started, they seemed to come out in a big stream, like when the recess bell goes and all the kids come flooding out. My words came running outside like it was the last day of school and I couldn't seem to stop them.

I don't know how long I babbled away, but there didn't seem to be any time limit and I'm pretty sure about three years of life escaped me before I remembered how to close my mouth. Once I finally stopped talking, it was her turn. I should say Julianna's turn. I actually knew her name all along but had been too rude to use it, even in my head. She was actually pretty nice. Not that I want to sound like some kind of instant convert or anything, but I have to admit, she managed to make some sense and actually seemed to give a crap about me.

On that first day she mostly talked about lookingforlight. Julianna seemed to accept that LFL was my friend and didn't try to tell me I never really knew her just because I had never met her. She told me that friendships can exist in all different ways and that I had just as much right to grieve for her as I would if it were one of my school friends. She told me that my feelings were OK and that I would need to take the time to work through them all. That it was all right to miss LFL and that the pain I was feeling was normal. I almost smiled when she said the word normal. It was something my mom would have said. I didn't feel like screaming when Julianna said it, though. This time, I needed to hear that my emotions were normal. That someone dying makes you feel confused and crazy and in so much pain you want to curl up in a little ball and shut the whole world out. That the pain wouldn't always be this strong even though your feelings for the person would always be there. That maybe Time would finally be on my side and help me figure out those feelings so that I could feel OK about the world again some day. That some day I would think about her and it wouldn't make my throat ache and my stomach hurt, but that wouldn't mean that I didn't care about her anymore.

Julianna explained a lot more about what could have happened to LFL as well. She said that eating disorders can cause all kinds of problems like dehydration, malnutrition, low blood pressure, really slow heart rate, electrolyte imbalances, and hormonal imbalances that can all cause serious problems with the heart. She explained what it all meant in a way that was pretty clear and easy to understand. I know I read all about it before and learned about it at school, but this was different. This time I was talking about someone I knew. I had to understand it this time. I had to find a spot in my brain to store it so I wouldn't forget.

I kept expecting her to start talking about me and my eating and how I was doing everything wrong. But she didn't. This is going to sound weird, but I was a little disappointed even though I was relieved at the same time. More evidence that my mind was MIA. Anyway, it was just that I sort of thought we were going to talk about me. Well, we talked about me, but it was mostly about my feelings about LFL.

So, I surprised myself by making a couple of extra appointments to talk to her about other stuff. I didn't know exactly what stuff I was going to talk about, but I was starting to believe that a little more talking might help me to start thinking again someday without my head hurting.

June 1

Sitting outside in the chilly morning air, it felt more like April 1st than June 1st. I used to hate April Fools' Day because I couldn't stand the thought that someone might pull a practical joke on me. I hate practical jokes. I like to be in control of things and when someone fakes me out I feel like a fool, which is not a nice feeling. Why is there a day designed to make fun of people? It seems kind of mean.

After days of thinking and talking and listening and listening and talking and thinking, I didn't know for sure what I was anymore. Sometimes I felt like life was a big practical joke with me at the brunt of it and everyone else laughing at my expense. Like I thought I had control over everything in my life and suddenly found out that I didn't have control over *anything*. The ultimate fool.

At other times I felt like I just needed to get some perspective on life. Maybe I just needed more real information so that I could maybe understand more about things. I was starting to think that there was a possibility that having control didn't necessarily mean figuring it all out alone. Maybe having control meant knowing when to find someone to help you with some of the figuring out. Someone who wasn't right in the middle of trying to figure out the exact same things you were. Someone who could maybe stand on the outside of your shadow and help you see yourself a little more clearly. Maybe the fool is the one who is standing alone, trying to find out the answers all by herself.

"Hi." I looked up into the sunlight. Marina and Wolf were both standing there. I hadn't talked to either of them for days. Any time either of them had tried to see me, I had just said I was busy and they both finally gave up and left me alone for a while. Not exactly the champion of keeping friendships. I had been so immersed in my own thoughts that I hadn't even tried to talk to anyone but Julianna.

"Hi," I answered. I was glad to see them standing there in the sun and even gladder that they still wanted to see me after so much time had passed. With my recent track record friend-wise, I would not have been surprised if they had both given up completely. I needed a friend or two. Or maybe three.

"We figured since you were actually outside again, you might be ready to see us," Wolf said.

"Would 'how are you' be a stupid question?" Marina asked.

"Probably." I kind of smiled. Not a full wattage one, but a bit of a face stretch.

"How are you?" she asked. This time I actually smiled.

"I don't actually know – yet. I still feel sad and angry and confused. I feel like I lost a big piece of myself. Like I have this big hole in my gut that makes everything hurt all of the time."

"She was your friend," Marina said, summarizing it all in one simple statement.

I smiled again. I should have known she would get it.

"That's what Julianna said too. I guess there are all kinds of friends. It scared me, you know? I mean, she was just like me. She just wanted to look good and feel good about herself. Now she's dead, and everything I was so sure about before doesn't seem to make as much sense to me as it used to."

"You don't need to be scared. You're talking things out. It takes more than a week or two to figure your life out. Julianna's cool. You'll be OK," Wolf said. I looked at him standing there, smiling at me with the light glistening in his hair and waited for my heart to flop. Nothing. Maybe I was just too full of mixed-up emotions to make room for romantic ones.

"I'm not so sure. It's been, like, a week and a half, and I still don't really know anything. I'm still a mess."

Marina looked at me and shook her head. "Well, try brushing your hair." She reached over and rubbed my head. I slapped her hand away and surprised myself by laughing.

"Thanks. I can always count on you for great advice."

"Seriously, give yourself a break here. You're trying. You've been talking to someone. Seeing as that's never exactly been your favorite thing to do here, that was tough enough. Give it some time."

"I've always hated time." Even as I said it I wondered if it was really true anymore. So many things were changing. Maybe my relationship with time was changing, too, and it might finally be on my side.

"Well, give it something you don't hate then. Anyway,

we're going for lunch and thought maybe you'd come with us now that you're actually out in public again. If you can call this place public."

"Lunch?"

"Yeah, it's that thing some people eat after breakfast and before supper." Marina shook her head at me again and grabbed my left hand. Wolf grabbed my right and they walked me down the hall, hand in hand in hand like three foolish little kids looking for worms as they head off for kindergarten. As I stumbled along between them, I felt a little lighter, like maybe Wolf was right and things might possibly turn out to be OK.

Later that day, as I sat on my bed trying to digest my attempt at eating a bit of lunch, it occurred to me that I had accidentally lied to Marina when I told her that I didn't know anything. When I looked inside my mind a little and sorted through the mess, I realized that I did know a few things. I took out my computer and started writing, just in case my brain took another holiday.

chapter 21

My name is Madison Nessfield, and I am living in a guest-house for young people with eating disorders while trying to find some of the missing fragments of my life. I am one of those complicated thousand-piece puzzles that takes a long time to put together, and I have a lot more work to do before I'm done. There are a few pieces already in place, though.

I know that I have to call Annie. There are people here who care for me, but I'm really going to need my best friend.

I know that I have to take time to show my mom the gardens next time she visits. I'm going to need my mom.

I know that I might even have to spend some time sitting in a circle making a few new friends. And I'll need to spend some more time talking about my life to a relative stranger so that I can leave here with more of me than I came in with.

And I know that when I do leave, I have to step out into the sunshine from time to time and cast my shadow on the ground so that I can remember who I've been, find out where I am, and have the courage to face what lies ahead.

Who knows? Maybe I'll find out that I'm a morning person after all.

To find out more visit www.thinandbeautiful.com

Liane Shaw's own battle with anorexia, as well as her role as a mother and a teacher, inspired her to write this story. She lives in Ontario, Canada.